Deadsweep

Beca Lewis

PERCEPTION PUBLISHING

Contents

ONE

For the last two weeks, I have walked through the meadow to the top of the hill and waited. I've watched the sun rise and fall, the clouds sweep through the blue sky, and the trees bend with the wind. I have watched the first spring flowers poking up from the ground with their promise that winter is almost over.

Every day I have searched the horizon for signs of their return. At the end of the day, I have walked back down to my father's home with even more unhappiness in my heart.

Four months have gone by since I returned to Erda. Four months since everything I ever knew turned upside down.

When I stepped through the portal from Earth to Erda, I had been stupid, untrained, ignorant, full of myself, and yet I was happy. Four months later I am a little less foolish and ignorant, a little more trained, and maybe still full of myself, but now I am unhappy.

There is no excuse for it, and yet I keep making excuses, which brings me back to thinking that I am full of myself. Or is it as Professor Link had said to me when we were in the Castle? That I thought I was superior? Do I still? Perhaps. Maybe it would be easier if I did.

Perhaps then I could embrace my future with open arms. I would claim my inheritance as future Queen of Erda and be comfortable now as Princess Kara Beth. I would let go of my past life as Hannah from Earth. I would rejoice in our victory over the Shrieks and Shatterskin.

Instead, all I could think was that after all that had happened, I was alone. Yes, we had saved Erda from the Shrieks and Shatterskin. Both of those monsters made by Abbadon were vanquished. But we knew that Erda's safety was temporary. Abbadon would be back. Abbadon would not give up trying to destroy magic, Erda, and every living thing but himself. We knew he was preparing another onslaught.

And yet, every day I walked to the top of that hill and waited. And when no one came and nothing changed, I returned to the city and my father, Darius, the King of Erda.

Today was no different. No one came. Even the Priscillas had deserted me. Pris, Cil, and La had become my constant companions, living in my pocket, pulling my hair. Laughing and pranking like the fairies that they are, I had come to rely on them. We had been friends since my childhood in Erda, and yet they had gone with the rest of them. Somewhere.

The only remaining member of our team that was still around was Lady, the pileated woodpecker that had come with me through the portal from Earth and then revealed herself as the woman I knew as Suzanne, and a dragon in Erda. So if Lady was with me, so was Suzanne. Except that she wasn't, because Lady had not transformed herself once since the rest of the team had gone on their fact-finding mission.

I had begged her. Literally. On my knees. Gone out into the woods and called Lady and asked her to please talk to me. Tell me what was going on. Please, shapeshift back to Suzanne so we can talk. Or stay as Lady and speak to me. But she remained silent, so I had no one to answer my questions.

Why didn't they take me? I didn't understand. I had been with them for months, fighting beside them, relearning magic. But one morning I woke up and they had all gone, every single one of them. All they left was a note that they would be back.

Even Zeid was gone. And that was the worst of all. We only had a few days together after I remembered who he was. My betrothed. Betrothed, an old word, still used in Erda. No wonder my heart had thudded the first time I saw him. I didn't remember him, but my heart had.

Before he left, we had spent time walking in the gardens of the city of Eiddwen. He told me how hard it had been for him since I had gone away. He said that he had been broken-hearted when I was sent to Earth to keep me safe from Abbadon. He told me his heart broke again when I returned to Erda and didn't remember him.

Now it is my heart that has broken. But I have duties to attend to. My father is not well, and with everyone gone, it is up to me to take care of him. If I was going to be honest with myself, I knew that was why I was left behind. I was the only one that had a chance to save King Darius. I had hoped that my return to Erda would bring him enough happiness to recover and rule his kingdom again.

When Shatterskin destroyed Ruta's village, my mother, Rowena, was one of the people that died there. When my father found out that his wife had died, he too started dying. The once proud man began to wilt. He had given up. He didn't want to live without his wife. I wanted him to live for his Kingdom and me. I wanted to believe that we would be enough for him.

My parents had lived as husband and wife for thousands of years, happily ruling over Erda with kindness and compassion. The people loved them, and my parents returned that love tenfold.

Thousands of years are not that long on Erda. People on Erda don't age past the age they chose to remain. I remember people in Earth saying that they would remain thirty-nine forever. It was a joke in the Earth Realm, in Erda it was true. Pick your age and stay there, slowly changing over a long, long time. The only way people died in Erda was by accident, someone killed them, or they decided to move on. That's what my father was doing, moving on. If he managed to accomplish it, I would be the ruler of Erda.

I didn't want to rule Erda. Not now. Not ever. I wanted my father to recover. My father's heart was broken not just because my mother had died, but it was because of his brother, Abbadon. Abbadon, the destroyer, the Evil One.

When the two brothers were first brought to Erda, they had agreed to rule their separate kingdoms and stay out of each other's way.

However, Abbadon didn't like sharing anything with his brother Darius even though there was plenty of room for both of them. Peace had reigned for centuries in my father and mother's Kingdom.

But as time passed, Abbadon became more and more invested in the dark side of greed and power, he had become dissatisfied at having only half of the planet. He wanted it all. And he was coming to get it.

The hill I climbed every day was behind the city to the East. I loved that hill. It was where we all had landed in the Sound Bubble after defeating the Shrieks and Shatterskin.

We had stood there together as a community. My friends. My teachers. We had looked at the sun glancing off the rooftops and celebrated our victory. We could see the people of Eiddwen waiting in the streets for us to celebrate with them.

For two days, it was glorious.

And then it was over. Everyone was gone. I had no idea when my friends would return, and Abbadon was advancing. I could do nothing alone. I needed them.

Two

The sky had turned gray to match my mood as I walked through the streets of Eiddwen back to our home where my father was now residing. Where he was supposed to be living was back at the Castle, as king. The same castle where I had lived after coming through the portal from the Earth dimension. But my father hadn't been there to greet me. As soon as my mother died, he had moved back to his family home to Eiddwen where he could pretend that he wasn't the King of Erda.

I could understand my father's grief, but still, the selfish part of me wondered why he didn't realize how much his support would have meant to me if he had waited for me at the Castle. I had lost someone too. Now, with my father lying half dead in bed because of his choices, it felt as if I had lost both of them.

At least some things were clearer to me now. I understood why the people who were waiting for me outside the Castle that first day didn't seem happy to see me.

I had known so little then. I hadn't known I was a princess, so I didn't understand why they reluctantly bowed to me. I found out much later that the people of Erda didn't know that I had been sent away to the Earth dimension by my parents. They thought I had deserted my parents and the Kingdom. They hadn't known that when I first returned, I had no memory of who I was and no access to any of my powers.

How could they have known? No one had told them. My father had deserted them by running away to his home in Eiddwen.

When I was sent to live in the Earth Realm, only a small group of people other than my parents had known. Even though my parents were not at the Castle to greet me, one being dead and the other running away, the others were there. Suzanne, Beru, Ruta, Niko, Aki, Professor Link, and of course Zeid, were waiting for me. They were the ones who had started my training to return to myself.

Now that the people of my father's kingdom knew my role in destroying the Shrieks and Shatterskin, they no longer greeted me with scowls, but with smiles and waves. I guess I had earned their respect. I wondered how easily I could lose it.

Despite my mood of sorrow, I loved walking the streets of Eiddwen. Eiddwen was like most of the villages in the Kingdom of Zerenity. It was large enough to be called a city, although a tiny city in my opinion. The streets were lined with charming small homes. Every home had gardens filled with flowers, herbs, and vegetables. Trees were everywhere, and a deep old growth forest lay on the other side of the meadow. All the power was supplied through the energy of the earth, so there was no need for wires or light fixtures. The people of Erda had learned long ago how to live as a partner within the graces of nature.

It was one reason that Abbadon wanted to destroy it. He did not believe in collaboration or community. Instead, he destroyed nature and then harvested the power and energy that he needed from the creatures of Erda that his monsters captured. He used them and then discarded them. The horror of that discovery would never leave me. What terrified me was that there were probably many more manufacturing plants in existence, other than the one we had destroyed.

I tabled that thought and arranged my face to be happy and pleased as I entered our home. This house wasn't any different from any other home in Eiddwen. There was no sign that the King of Erda lived here. That is, if you could call it living. My father had taken to staying in his bedroom all day staring at the ceiling, willing himself to leave.

Since my return, he had stabilized, but was not getting better. It was as if he was living in two places. I had to convince him to come back to Erda and help me save the Kingdom.

Once the people who took care of my father learned that I had not deserted them, but had been sent away, they stopped pretending that I was invisible, and I became the person they were most happy to see. That happiness had much to do with their desire that their King recover and the knowledge that I might help with that process. In the absence of my friends, I had come to rely on their friendly faces.

Today, my father's head of the house, Berta, met me at the front door and asked if she could speak to me in private before I went in to see my father.

I followed her to her office, a little room to the right of the front door. From there, Berta had a view of the street in front of the house, the front door, and all the hallways that led to the rest of the house. She also had a view of the kitchen because she had installed a window that looked into that room. Berta had her finger on the pulse of everything going on in that house.

Like every dwelling in Erda, the room's light changed as we entered her office to match what was needed. The trees handle all the lighting in my father's kingdom through their roots. This was unlike the homes of the beings that lived underground, where the tree roots are visible as they hold up the dirt walls. Homes in the towns do not have visible roots in the walls, but I know that they are there, anyway. Now that I had begun to understand the trees of Erda, it never fails to feel comforting to go into a room and feel their presence inside as much as outside.

Berta gestured to the chair in front of her desk made of a large slab of wood polished to perfection. Only one piece of paper was on it. If she needed anything, I knew Berta would wave her hand and it would be there. Berta was a master of practical magic. As I watched her sit behind the desk, I realized that even though Professor Link was not there to teach me more about magic, Berta was. I was embarrassed to realize how much time I had wasted by not taking advantage of what was around me.

I curled my feet up under me and waited. I could feel my heart race faster and faster as Berta merely sat and looked at me. It was the silence that was killing me. Back in the days when I was training at the Castle, almost all my teachers used the tool of silence on me, waiting for me to discover what I needed to find out, or make a fool of myself, and here Berta was using it on me now.

"I'm sorry, Berta," I said.

"What are you sorry for, Kara Beth?" Berta asked, not that unkindly. Berta reminded me of my friend Grace from the Earth dimension, and I wondered if they were related. That thought took me down another path. I remembered what Suzanne had told me about the same people being in different dimensions. What if Berta was the Grace of Erda?

I tabled that thought for the moment and answered, "For moping around wishing for what isn't instead of enjoying what is."

Berta stood and walked to my chair and gestured for me to stand up. Confused, I stood, afraid of what was going to happen next. Instead, Berta reached out and pulled me into a hug, just like the ones that Grace used to give me.

I burst into tears and sobbed just like a little girl. Berta held me and patted me on my back, saying, "There, there, let it out, little one."

Hearing her say little one made me cry even harder. I had been trying to be so grown up, and yet in my heart, I yearned to just be loved because I was me, and not because I was supposed to save the

Kingdom. It was a relief to be only Hannah from the Earth Realm, or even just Kara Beth, instead of a princess.

When I was all cried out, Berta produced a cool cloth, which she simply plucked from the air, and dabbed it all over my face. I hadn't felt so good in ages.

"Okay, now we can go see your father. It's time for both of you to stop pining away and start living again."

When I started to say thank you, she shook her head and said, "Not necessary, my dear."

She held my hand, and we walked down the hall to my father's room together. Berta was right. It was time to start living in Erda. I was ready.

THREE

Berta and I found Darius in bed with all the drapes closed and a washcloth across his eyes. It was precisely how I expected him to be because that was what he looked like every day. The man I remembered, whose presence was so huge that it filled rooms when he walked in, was no longer there. He had been replaced with a shriveled version of a man.

When I first returned home, I had some sympathy for my father. I tried to understand why he didn't bother to greet me, just lay in a dark room, barely breathing. After all, he had lost his wife.

But once my friends deserted me, and my father made no effort to talk to me or get better, I found myself getting mad at him. It was his choice to leave, to let himself become a shrunken version of the man that he used to be.

Being angry at my father didn't make me like myself very much, but as hard as I tried to let it go, I couldn't get the resentment to go away. Every morning I would stop in his room and say hello. Hold his hand. Tell him I had returned.

At night, I sat with him and read from one of his favorite books. But he didn't acknowledge me at all. I wanted to scream at him. "Here I am, your daughter. Why are you choosing to leave me? Why are you not helping save your kingdom? Abbadon wants to destroy all life on the planet, for zuts sake!"

Sometimes, I would remind him that I lost someone too. I lost my mother in Erda and all my friends in the Earth dimension. I couldn't understand it. How could he desert me? How could he abandon his people?

As we stood in the doorway together, I knew that Berta wanted me to try again to reach him. I was willing to try to give up my anger and resentment, but was he willing to let go of feeling sorry for himself? Berta gave my hand a last squeeze and left me to enter the room by myself, but not before whispering to me that it was alright to be mad, and perhaps I should tell him why I was. It might help us both.

When I looked at her to make sure I had heard what she said correctly, she gave me an encouraging nod before returning to her office.

I stood by my father's bedside, looking at the man in the bed. No, he didn't look anything like the father I remembered, but that I remembered him at all was something to be happy about.

Until recently, I hadn't even remembered my mother and father's name, let alone my life with them. Being sent away to live in the Earth dimension had wiped my memory of all things Erda, including my parents and all the other people I loved. Over time, some of my memory and magical skills had returned. For that, I was very grateful.

I pulled a chair up beside the bed and started talking. I told my father everything that had happened since I came through the portal and returned to Erda. How I almost died inside of the monster Shatterskin but was saved because my friend La had escaped and brought help.

I told him about my time in the Castle, where he was supposed to be, and the training I had received from Niko, Aki, and Professor Link.

I described the help that the Ginete had been in building shields so we could get close enough to dissolve the Shrieks. I told him about how the Whistle Pigs had dug a hole big enough to drop the disabled Shatterskin down into the earth where he could never hurt anyone again.

Describing the manufacturing plants where Abbadon made the Shrieks by draining his prisoners of all their life force brought me to tears. We rescued some of them, but hundreds more had died. I told him how happy I had been when Leif and Sarah had stepped out of the Sound Bubble and embraced me. How for two days all of us celebrated together. And then a few days later, all of them were gone, leaving me alone in Eiddwen.

By the time I was done telling him the whole story, I was exhausted. But more than that, I was furious, and I told him so.

"What right do you have to give up? The fight is not over. Mother would never, ever, have given up like you are!" I screamed at him.

The figure on the bed didn't move. "You can't possibly be my father," I whispered to him. "You don't look like him. He would never leave his Kingdom and me this way. Whoever you are, I give up. My father must already be dead."

Something inside of me broke when I said those words. It was true. The man in the bed could not be the King. I could not waste one more minute of my life moping around because whoever was lying there refused to live.

There was a light knock on the door, and one of the women who took care of the man on the bed poked her head in the door and asked if she could come in.

"It's okay," I said. "I'm done here." And I meant it. My father had made a choice.

Now I had to make one too, and it was not going to be the same one he was making. I was going to stop moping around. I was not going to wait until everyone returned. I would resume my training with whom and what I had.

But it would have to be the next day. Telling my father the story, and then making my decision to let him be, had wiped me out. Too tired to eat, I stumbled into my bedroom and fell into bed without bothering to take off my clothes.

Right before I fell asleep, I whispered a little prayer that all my friends were safe, and just before sleep took over I thought I heard Leif's voice, telling me that all was well.

Berta must have come in during the night and covered me, because when I woke up I was snuggled under the covers, still clothed, but no longer angry. I was determined.

If I had to be Queen, I would be. But first, there was a monster to rid the world of, and I needed to be prepared. And I knew just what I needed to do.

Four

Berta was waiting for me in the small breakfast nook tucked into a corner of the kitchen. Food was already on the table, and a cup of steaming hot coffee was waiting for me. I had no idea how coffee ended up in Erda, but I was delighted that it did. On the other hand, Berta was the queen of practical magic. Perhaps she just pulled it out of the air.

When Berta laughed at me, I knew she had heard what I was thinking, and maybe that was what she had done. It was time for me to access the resources I had at my fingertips and Berta was the place to start.

"Didn't get very far with your father, did you?" Berta said, slipping into a chair opposite me. We were the only two at the table. Caretakers came and went in the house during the day, but the two of us and my father were the only ones that lived there. Berta took care of everything. I knew nothing about how things worked in the "real world" of doing things in Erda.

Since I had returned to Erda, other than the two weeks I had been moping around my father's house, I had been training to fight monsters. That was not your everyday kind of living. It was certainly not the kind of life that I had lived in the Earth Realm.

But since my return to Erda, I hadn't had much time to learn the basics of Erda living. Sure, I had an excuse, but it sucked. And I was tired of myself and the excuses. What I had decided after talking to my father was burning inside of me.

It could have been anger. But my friends Niko and Beru taught me how to use anger, and that was what I was going to do.

"Nowhere, Berta, but it helped me to tell him everything, just as you said that it would. It helped me make a decision."

"What decision was that?" Berta asked as she pulled the most amazing-smelling cinnamon rolls out of the oven.

The steam from the stove made her little gray curls that were peeping out from the cap she wore on her head curl a bit more. She slapped my hand as I reached for a bun even before she had a chance to put them on my plate. What can I say? I was hungry from not eating the night before.

"To train. While I was at the Castle, Professor Link taught me magic. Niko taught me how to fight and defend myself, and Aki taught me how to be calm, still, and listen. At least that was their primary focus, although everyone was trying to teach me.

"Since they left me here in Eiddwen, I haven't done anything other than mope around wanting them to come back. However, it's been radio silence. I haven't heard anything from anyone.

"Last night I remembered that they all used silence on me from time to time. They sometimes left me alone until I figured something out on my own. So, what if that is what they are doing now?

"Sure, they could be out researching what Abbadon is doing. But they didn't need to all go. My fairy friends, the Priscillas could have stayed. Or even Beru, or maybe Ruta. For sure, Cahir could have stayed with me.

"Why would a wolf need to go with them? But they all left except Lady who won't talk to me. Why would that be unless it is because they want me to do something while they are gone?"

"What do you think they want you to do?" Berta asked. I didn't know Berta that well, but I could have sworn I saw her try to stifle a laugh. It was okay. I deserved to be laughed at.

"Train on my own. Starting with you!"

This time Berta did start laughing. She laughed so long I started worrying that she would never stop. When she finally gathered herself together, her face was bright pink, and tears were running down her cheeks.

If anyone else had laughed at me like that, I would have gotten huffy and either stomped out of the room or started crying. It all depended on who had done the laughing.

Instead, I stared at her, and then as calmly as possible asked her why she was laughing.

"Oh, my darling girl," Berta said. "I can't teach you anything that you don't already know. But I appreciate the thought that you think I can. However, I do believe you are on the right track with the listening piece. And the decision to stop moping is a great one.

"Your father may or may not recover. There is nothing you can do now but be willing for it to be okay with you either way. And I think you came to that decision last night, didn't you?"

I nodded at her, and she patted my hand as she put another roll onto my plate. She put the rest of the food onto a platter which I knew was for anyone who came to the house that day. No one went hungry in Berta's home.

I stared at the roll, wondering if I had room to eat it or if I was making a pig of myself. Like all of Berta's cooking, they were delicious.

"If I were you, I would eat up. I think you are heading for a busy day. I'll be in the garden if you need me."

I remained in the kitchen finishing my roll and coffee and thinking about what Berta had said. If she wasn't going to train me, I would have to teach myself. I wondered if that's what she meant when she said I was heading for a busy day.

Today I was not going to the hill to wait all day for people who may not come. They would return someday, and they would be disappointed in me if all I did was wait for them.

Instead, I was going to see what I could do on my own. If I had to fight Abbadon's new monster by myself, I would. I said that to myself with all the bravado I could muster. At the same time, I knew that my friends, the team that had defeated the Shrieks and Shatterskin with me, would return and they would want me to be ready.

I decided to begin the day the same way I would have done if they were there. In quiet meditation. Berta had shown me a small side garden that she told me my mother, Rowena, had used every morning. There was a tiny hut inside the enclosure that she used when it was raining or snowing, but otherwise, she placed a mat on the grass and sat there.

After changing into clean clothes and brushing my hair back into a ponytail, I opened the door to the meditation garden. I could almost feel my mother's presence. It was the perfect place for me to begin.

FIVE

That day was the turning point for my time in Eiddwen. I had made a decision. I could still be Hannah who felt loved and cared for by the people in the Earth Realm while becoming the strong woman I knew I had to be in Erda. I would embrace the fact that in Erda I am Princess Kara Beth.

I developed a training routine based on what I had learned during my time at the Castle. Since no one was going to do it with me, I could do it myself.

Niko had taught me that having a routine helped to accomplish anything, so I made one for myself that I was determined to follow every day no matter what the weather was, or how I felt.

First, I visited my father every morning on my way to breakfast. I stopped to read to him every evening on my way to bed, no matter how tired I had made myself that day. I worked on not letting myself get pulled into what he was doing.

Although it was ironic that while I was building a routine to make myself better, my father had developed a method to make himself worse. Every morning I wondered if he would still be there when I went to visit in the evening. The fact that he was still hanging on gave me a modicum of hope that he would recover, but I wasn't expecting it or waiting for it.

After seeing my father in the morning, I had breakfast with Berta and filled her in on what I had done the day before. If she hadn't been there, I am sure I would have gone crazy.

Until then, I hadn't realized how much it meant to me to share my experience. It gave me a purpose. It helped me remember why I was doing what I was doing. Berta listened better than anyone I had ever known, except for maybe Grace from the Earth dimension.

The more time I spent with Berta, the more she reminded me of Grace. They looked almost the same. They both had dark brown eyes that looked deep inside and found goodness in everyone. And I needed to know that there was goodness in me.

Like Grace, who knew everyone in the village, so did Berta. Both loved to cook and serve others, and both gave great hugs. Even if Berta wasn't Grace in the realm of Erda, she made me feel the same. Loved and cared for. And that made all the difference to me because the routine I set for myself was hard and became harder as the days went by.

Truth be told, I was hoping that someday, when I saw my friends again, they would all be proud of me. However, I tried not to make that the main reason because I knew that it would lead me down a dangerous path. I needed to train for myself, and for the people of the Kingdom of Zerenity.

After breakfast, I spent over an hour in my mother's garden, listening mostly. I quieted my mind the best that I could and then waited. Some days I never did get myself to be quiet, and other days I was filled with so many feelings that I would find myself crying throughout the entire hour.

I knew I couldn't make one experience better than another. Even though I preferred those magical times when I could feel the earth breathe through me, that didn't make them better than the days I had to fight to be calm. Because if I thought that, I wasn't listening. I was judging.

However, my favorite mornings in the garden were when I felt my mother's presence. It was as if she had left little love notes for me there that I would run into every once in a while. Not physical ones. But thoughts don't go away just because someone is not with us anymore. Or that's what Aki had told me, and I believed her.

Thoughts hang around waiting for someone to read them or tune into them. I knew my mother had left those love notes for me deliberately, hoping that someday I would come to the garden and collect them.

I left her little love notes there too, just in case she was somewhere she could receive them. One can hope, can't they?

Berta would pack me a light lunch because she knew that I would be out all day and probably not be back to the house until dinner. My lunch was always waiting for me in the kitchen after my hour in the garden. The rest of the day varied. I practiced some of the moves that Niko had taught me. Without a sparring partner, it was more difficult, but I did it anyway.

Aki had worked with me to improve my range of movement, and I spent time doing many of the yoga forms that she had taught me.

After that, I ran. I altered where I ran. Some days, I ran through the woods and tried to clear the way through the trees the way that Ruta would do. That didn't work. Maybe only Ruta's people, who looked like tree stumps if you looked at them with squinted eyes, could do that.

It was probably for the best that I couldn't because I started to learn how to run without tripping over my own feet. Sometimes I swear the trees dropped their branches so I would learn to duck, and raised their roots so I would pay attention. I thought I heard them laugh at me, but I didn't mind. The trees were my companions. I knew that the trees provided all the magic and life that made up Erda.

Other days, I ran through the streets into the meadow and then up the hill. It took a long time for me to get up that hill without stopping and trying to breathe without passing out. It helped to pretend that Beru, my little elf-like friend who looked like a flower, was with me. I would imagine her holding my hand and her long legs effortlessly pulling me up the hill. At the top, I would pause, take in the city of Eiddwen, thank Beru for running with me, and head back down. How many times I tripped and fell on the way down was ridiculous, but after a few weeks of training, I was running more like Beru and less like the clumsy person I was before.

Some days I saw Lady circling above my head. Usually, she flew by herself, but once in a while a whole crown of dragons would fly by and dip their black and white wings at me, and my heart would lift in gratitude. I was still being watched over, even if no one was talking to me. I knew they would, in time, and I would be ready.

SIX

Each day, before the day was over, I did one more thing. Maybe it was the most important thing, but I tried not to make it feel that way. I practiced feeling and using my gifts of magic.

Right before we defeated Shatterskin, I had remembered most of the magical gifts that I had. Not all of them. But I had remembered how to shoot lightning bolts, and how to fly short distances. I wanted to do so much more than that, but I had to start with what I had remembered and improve those abilities.

Since the day I shot lightning bolts out of my hands to convince the people of Beru's village that there was a danger they needed to prepare for, I could use that skill to a greater or lesser degree.

I had used it, with the Priscillas' help, to dissolve the batteries inside of Shatterskin and light balls of tree sap with it. However, since then the lightning out of my hands wasn't always available.

I didn't want to have to be angry or afraid to make my magic work. What I wanted was to be able to control it when I needed it, even if it was only to light a fire.

I had plans. I was going to travel to the Castle on my own, and I knew I needed to know how to start a campfire. It would seem that if I could shoot lightning bolts, lighting fires would be an easy thing to do. Right. Not at all.

There were days that nothing happened. I breathed, prayed, listened, stamped my feet, yelled, cried, and that little pile of wood

I had set beside the woods outside of Eiddwen just stared back at me. Yes, stared back at me, mocking me.

Then other days I would stretch out my hand, the same way I had seen Beru light a fire, and "poof," there it was. I'm not sure which made me more frustrated—the times that it didn't work, or the times that it did—because I had no idea how it was happening when it did work, or why it wouldn't work the other times.

Flying was the same. Some days I could leap and fly through the trees, and other days, nothing. Even though using magical skills was not consistent for me, I was determined to be persistent in my practice.

When I shared my frustration with Berta, she would tell me to be patient. Perhaps it wasn't time yet. When she said that, I knew that she knew I was going to leave, with or without my friends.

I needed to find out what was happening with Abbadon. The only way I knew to do that was to start walking back to the Castle and talk to the people I met along the way to find out what was going on in the Kingdom.

Without Professor Link's communication channel in my head, I felt almost blind. I used to be upset that people were always listening in and talking to me in my head. Now I would give anything to have all of those voices back.

One morning Berta asked me if I had met the people of Eiddwen yet. If I was preparing to meet other people in my walk across the Kingdom, why not start at home?

It was times like that when I discover that I am still an idiot. How could I have missed that part? That day I added time in my training to meet people. I walked the streets of Eiddwen and talked to people working in their gardens. I joined the kids playing in the streets. I went to the stores and bought the supplies that Berta needed to run my father's house.

I sat in the parks and talked to whoever came to sit beside me. The more I met the people, the more I wanted to know all about them. I started knocking on doors and introducing myself as Hannah. I didn't want to be Princess Kara Beth, possibly the future Queen Kara Beth. I wanted to be a member of the village.

They knew I wasn't just Hannah. Even though I hadn't remembered them, they remembered me. But they all pretended along with me that Hannah was who I was. I ate with them. I held their newborn babies. I learned how to feed the chickens, plant the next crop of lettuce, and make a decent pot of soup. Along the way, I stopped yearning for what I didn't have and found that the more love I gave the people, the more joy I felt.

No one said anything about Abbadon. I wasn't looking for information about him. When I left, it would be time enough to learn more about his evil ways. My time in Eiddwen was about relearning about the good ways.

Yes, I must have known these things when I had lived in Erda before I was sent to the Earth dimension. Yes, I had experienced the good ways in the Earth Realm, but I hadn't known that I could find them no matter where I was. I hadn't known how easy it was to find the good ways in every culture and every dimension.

I still wore the star necklace that Liza, the girl from Beru's village, gave to me. I knew that if I touched it, I would see the world differently. I would be able to see the 4D of it. But Aki's warning to me to not use it just because I was curious had stuck with me.

I practiced trying to see differently without it and once in a while, I could. I could see the intertwining of all nature as one. I trusted that when I needed more, it would come to me. I added that to my daily practice.

Finally, almost six weeks later, I was ready. I had learned to light a fire with my magic (besides, I was bringing matches just in case magic failed) and my body was strong and healthy. I had replaced the loneliness in my heart with the love I felt for the people of Eiddwen and for the people I had yet to meet in the Kingdom of Zerenity. I missed my friends. My heart longed to see Zeid again, but if the time was not right for those two things, who was I to change what was supposed to happen?

Although no one talked about what Abbadon was doing, I could feel it. I could feel a dark force heading once again across the desolate land that the Shrieks and Shatterskin had destroyed. I could feel the death it brought with it. I had to meet it and stop it. If I had to walk back to the Castle on my own, I would.

One warm day in late May, I said goodbye to my father. He hadn't changed, but I had. If I never saw him again, I wanted him to know that no matter what; I loved him. I kissed his forehead and backed out of the room, taking in the shriveled man on the bed, hoping that one day the King in him would return.

Berta had helped me pack a backpack the night before. When she put a change of clothes in it, Berta was letting me know that she knew I was leaving in the morning. There was nothing to say. I had no words to tell her how much I loved her and would miss her.

I couldn't promise her I would be back. I couldn't promise her I would, or could, save the Kingdom. I could only promise her I was ready to try.

SEVEN

I had arrived in Eiddwen by Sound Bubble. It had taken no time at all to get there from the Castle. Getting back to the Castle was going to take much longer.

For one thing, I wanted to stop at Beru's village and see the people there. Liza's father James had told me that the town of Kinver would always be a home to me. A home where I could be Hannah and not Princess Kara Beth.

When we were fighting Shatterskin, Kit, one of the men from the village had died, so I also wanted to thank the people of Kinver for his help. In Erda, people's ashes were scattered to the wind once they moved through the open door called death, so there wasn't a gravesite to visit. But Kit's spirit and his family would still be there.

On the way out of Eiddwen, I stopped at the top of the hill and looked back. It was a beautiful city, and I was looking forward to visiting again soon. Surprisingly I had found happiness there. A few people stood in the streets looking up at the hill at me. I waved, and they waved back. After one last look, I turned and headed east.

I had decided not to take the road to Kinver. Instead, I wanted to walk through the woods. I had never done this on my own before, but it felt like the right thing to do. Berta had told me to look for the silver trail that would lead me to a stream that flowed southeast. She said to follow the stream's flow, and it would take me to Kinver.

The words "silver trail" didn't mean anything to me, but I trusted Berta would not lead me astray. After waving goodbye, I walked to the edge of the woods and looked for the silver trail.

I could have touched the star on my neck, and I knew that would show me the path, but the point of all this training was to be able to access these abilities without resorting to using outside help. I would use the star in an emergency, but this wasn't one. I had time.

Since I had been left alone in Eiddwen, I had learned to be much more comfortable with myself. With Berta's help, I had gained more trust that what I needed would come to me. When I hadn't seen the trail after standing at the edge of the woods for an hour, I found a nearby rock, or the rock found me, and I sat down and waited some more. Expectant. I knew the path was there. I just couldn't see it—yet.

I listened. I felt the rock, the ground, the trees, the sky, and the insects scuttling by my feet. I was in no hurry. I was where I was supposed to be. I squashed the part of me that wanted to complain, to roll my eyes at the delay. I waited with my eyes closed, feeling the sun warm my face.

I heard Beru's voice from the past say to me, "Feel it, Hannah, just as you did before you came here. Feel the forest. Feel the ground beneath your feet. Feel what all of nature has to give you. Reach out. Let all of life in."

When I felt completely at peace, I opened my eyes and saw it—a silver trail leading into the woods.

But I saw something else that made me leap up with joy, grab my backpack, and run as fast as I could to the woods edge.

I wouldn't be traveling alone after all.

He sat there as if it was the most natural thing in the world. That it wasn't a big deal for him to be there, even though I hadn't seen him since the defeat of Shatterskin.

He sat there while I ran straight at him. Didn't move while I grabbed him around the neck so hard we both ended up rolling on the ground—me with my face buried in his gray fur, trying not to cry. Cahir let me, remaining as dignified as he could with a human girl clutching his neck.

"Where have you been, Cahir?" I asked as soon as I could start talking. I was sitting cross-legged on the ground, and Cahir was lying there looking at me with his gold wolf eyes.

"Waiting for you here by the silver trail," Cahir pushed into my mind.

"All this time?" I asked him.

Cahir showed me that after Shatterskin's death he had gone to visit his family, traveling with his wolf pack that had come to help that day. He knew that I would be well taken care of at the Castle and didn't need him for a while. After a nice visit, and siring another round of wolf pups, he had come to Eiddwen to wait for me.

"Why didn't you come into the village? Or at least show yourself to me when I was waiting on the hill, or running up the dang blasted thing. I could have used a friend then."

"I was your friend then, Princess. If you had needed help, I was there. But what you needed most was to feel confident and capable on your own. When you were ready, I knew you would see the silver trail, and me here waiting for you."

One of the gifts visiting the Oracle had restored to me was being able to hear Cahir's thoughts. That I still could filled me with happiness. And now I could walk through the woods with him to Beru's village. Not alone. With Cahir.

"Well, I'm here too," I heard Lady's voice. She was talking to me again. How could I be any happier? I had passed some kind of test, and my friends were back. Nothing could be more glorious than that.

Except in my heart, I knew that the reason I had been tested was that I would need every skill that I had to be able to face Abbadon's new monster. All I knew about it was that it would do what Abbadon wanted all his monsters to do. Kill life. Any life. Anywhere.

For Abbadon, sweeping through the Kingdom of Zerenity with death would be the ultimate pleasure.

I planned on denying him that pleasure. And now I had help, and I was going to get more.

EIGHT

With Lady drumming ahead of us letting us know that everything was safe, Cahir beside me, and the silver thread to guide us, I felt as if heaven had opened up and embraced me. After two months of being by myself, just having Lady and Cahir back with me was almost enough for me to forget that there was still a dangerous madman out there in Erda.

Cahir and I walked together side by side through the forest, taking time to enjoy the sounds and feelings that existed there in harmony. Cahir was silent. Once I realized that no amount of questioning would get him to answer where the rest of the team had gone, I relaxed and walked. The trees gave me a break and didn't drop their branches or raise their roots, so I could drift along enjoying. I knew they were giving me a gift and I gave thanks for it.

That night, I gathered a moss bed as I had seen Ruta do countless times as we traveled together. I made a fire the same way I had seen Beru do it. I gathered the wood, and then stretched out my hand and lit it. This was work that I had not done before because the team had done it for me. By the time it was time to sleep, I was so tired I could barely pull a layer of leaves over me to keep warm. Beru would do that for me when we traveled together, and I missed her even more.

As I drifted off to sleep, with Cahir lying next to me keeping watch and Lady nesting in a tree above us, I realized once again how spoiled I had been when I arrived in Erda. Everything had been done for me. Perhaps that was how it had to be because I remembered nothing about Erda or my role in saving the Kingdom. I had no magic to speak of, and I was homesick and irritable the minute I picked myself off the ground after tripping over my own feet within seconds of coming through the portal.

No wonder they had left me alone for a few months. If they hadn't, I would still be expecting to be taken care of as if I was a child. I'm not going to lie, though. I wouldn't have minded getting taken care of again by Ruta and Beru. Or maybe I could reverse the roles and take care of them, once in a while.

When I woke up with the sunrise peeking through the trees, Cahir was already pacing around the now dead fire waiting for me so we could get moving. Unlike the day before, Cahir seemed restless. One thing I hadn't learned to do was have food appear out of nowhere. But Berta had packed lots of water and food bars for me—yes, once again being taken care of—so I was ready to start walking as soon as I returned the moss and the leaves where I had found them.

I threw dirt on the fire and scattered the wood. Beru could sweep her hand across the fire and put it out. I hadn't figured that one out yet.

"What's the big rush, Cahir?" I asked. "For two months, no one seemed to be in a big hurry to get me anywhere, and now we are hurrying."

Keeping pace with a trotting wolf is not easy, but I was doing my best. Good thing I had practiced running or I would have been completely exhausted within an hour with the pace he was keeping. Even so, after a few hours of full out running for me, and a leisurely pace for Cahir, I begged him to let me stop and rest.

He hadn't answered me when I asked about our increased speed. He just ignored the question. I recognized that tactic. It had been used on me quite effectively before. Pretend that nothing was said, and then it wasn't necessary to answer anything.

Breathing hard, hands on my knees, I'm sure I looked ridiculous to a bird or a wolf. I was trying to understand about breathing in the power that existed as part of all living things. However, I was still a novice, and not afraid to admit it.

"Come on, Cahir, what's the rush?"

"Do you still see the silver thread?" Cahir pushed into my mind.

"Sure. It looks brighter, though. Does that mean we are getting closer to where we are going?"

Cahir looked at me the way Niko sometimes looked at me. Disappointed. "Aren't you curious where it came from? Who made it? Why?"

Huh. Cahir was right. I hadn't asked. Just assumed it was part of another magic thing that I didn't understand. I took it for granted that it was there for me.

"You know that sometimes what looks like a path for you to take, will lead you astray, don't you?" Cahir said. If a wolf could huff, that's what he did.

"Are you telling me this path is like that? Why are we following it then?" I huffed right back.

"No. I am simply asking you why you didn't question it before you started following it. Next time it might mean life or death to you. But, yes, this one is for us."

"Okay, I'll bite. How was this trail made, and why are we rushing?"

"Because if I don't get you to the end of it soon, someone is going to be very unhappy with me, and I hate it when they pull my ears."

Nothing more needed to be said. I started running. Tried channeling Beru leading me, breathing in, feeling the power around me, and letting myself be part of it. I knew who had made the path, and who was waiting for me at the end of it.

I heard Lady's laughter up ahead. I felt Cahir chuckling to himself as we ran. And then I heard the tinkling laughter I had missed so much. Tears of joy were already running down my face even before I saw them.

The Priscillas were waiting by the stream, but as soon as we came into view they flew straight towards me, and I could barely stop myself from grabbing each one and covering them with kisses. Instead, I sat down on the floor of the forest and let them pull my hair, tweak my ears, and give me fairy kisses. All the while I sat there sobbing and laughing at the same time.

The Priscillas were back. Pris with her pig tales, Cil with her green eyes, and La with the white streak in her hair.

When I could finally speak, I said, "So you made the silver trail? That means Berta knows you?"

"Of course she does. Remember, we lived in Eiddwen too."

"But that means she spoke with you?"

The three Priscillas looked at each other and back at me, but didn't answer. What weren't they telling me?

NINE

Having the Priscillas tucked into my pockets and Cahir walking beside me made me so happy I was almost okay with the fact that neither Cahir nor the Priscillas would tell me anything about what they had been doing the last few months.

We reminisced about our time together—the time before they dropped me off and left me at Eiddwen. They darted around the subject, speaking instead about the dissolving of the Shrieks and the disabling of Shatterskin. I understood. I didn't want to relive the part before that, either.

When I asked how the Ginete and Whistle Pigs were doing, all I got back from Pris was the answer. "Fine." That affirmed to me that they were also involved in what was going on.

I wondered if Teddy and his Whistle Pig friends were under our feet right now building tunnels and magic circles to bring us down into the cozy underground homes they created for themselves and their cousins, the Ginete.

Pita and his four brothers, along with the Whistle Pigs, had housed and cared for us when we were fighting Abbadon's monsters. They were instrumental in defeating the Shrieks and Shatterskin, but not as fighters. Instead, the Ginete and Whistle Pigs are a cross between the Red Cross, faith ministers, and scientists, which made them invaluable in our battle with Abbadon's monsters. They supported and healed us while making the technology that enabled us to defeat the Shatterskin and his minions, the Shrieks.

Teddy reminded me of a big teddy bear with two big front teeth. That could have been scary, but his kind nature and habit of calling me funny names made him one of the warmest beings I had ever met.

When I had first met the Ginete, I was torn between thinking they were adorable with their big heads and huge golden eyes, and afraid of them because they were so serious. But it turned out that Pita and his brothers were not only brilliant, and the holders of the many magical secrets, but lovers of laughing.

Pita laughed holding his ears. I have no idea why, but I loved the picture of it. He could always get me going. When I learned that his mother named the five of them, Pita, Tita, Bita, Lita, and Sam, we both laughed so hard I felt like holding my ears too. I had told Pita I wanted to meet the mother who had to name her last son Sam because she couldn't think of another four-letter name that rhymed with Pita. I hadn't met her yet. Maybe one day soon.

"Are more people meeting us as we go along?" I casually threw into the conversation when we stopped for lunch.

"What people?" Cil asked, looking at me over the flower sandwich she was eating. At least it looked like a flower sandwich. However, the fact that there also appeared to be something wiggling inside of it made me glance away. Fairies are sweet looking, but don't piss one off.

I've been at the receiving end of Pris's little battering fists, which can really hurt. She had other ways to punish, too. More than once, Pris has shunned me because I said the wrong thing, or asked the wrong question.

When the three of them would go off on their own at night while we were staying underground, and I had asked them what they were doing, Pris stopped talking to me. She said that it was because I didn't trust them.

That wasn't it at all. I am just perpetually curious. On the other hand, I can be controlling too. I know that about myself. It doesn't mean that I like to be that way. I'm trying to let that part of my personality go. However, I admit that being controlling was what I was doing with that question, and I hadn't fooled Pris one bit.

It turned out that the three of them had been rounding up some weird brown insect friends of theirs who ate the remaining green globs, removing the Shrieks from the landscape forever.

I had apologized over and over again, and supposedly was forgiven, but I have been worried ever since that Pris is still slightly miffed at me. I don't want to get my head pounded again or lose her to one of her pouting sessions.

The problem is, the Priscillas read my mind. Well, everyone does. Read minds that is. So learning to keep my mind closed to unwanted peeking was a skill I was still learning. I had learned that there were channels, and I could close one, and open others. I always left the common channel that Professor Link communicated to the team on, just in case, but so far that had been silent for two months.

So Cil's innocent question, "What people?" was a landmine question. I decided to play it safe and ask if I would see Zeid soon. I thought they would understand why I asked that. After all, he was my fiancée or betrothed. Shouldn't I know where he was?

Pris answered the question, "No."

"No, what?" I know, perhaps I shouldn't have asked again. It was chancy to open my mouth since it was Pris who had said, "No."

"Zounds," Pris said wrinkling her pretty forehead which made the tiny star mark that lived there shrivel up into a dot, "Can't you just let things play out? Do you have to know everything? Why not just enjoy the walk to Kinver with us?"

It was La who came to my rescue. She rarely stood up to her big sister, but this time she did. "Why not let her know something?" she asked.

We all waited. Even Cahir waited. Would Pris tell me, or twist my hair, or pull Cahir's ears, or fly off in a pout?

Pris didn't do any of those things. Instead, she started laughing and did a little jig on my head. Stepping off my head so that she was flying directly in front of my face, she tweaked my nose and said, "Yes. There are some of our friends waiting for us at the village of Kinver."

When I started to ask who they were, she held up her hand. "No more questions. I don't care how curious you are. I'm not telling."

I smiled at Pris and said, "Thank you," but that didn't stop me from being so curious I thought I would burst. Who was going to be there? If not Zeid, who?

TEN

The overwhelming urge to continue to harass my friends for more information started to fade as the day wore on. Nature's beauty can soothe even the most controlling person–not saying that's me, and this was a day no one would be able to resist.

It was one of those beautiful late spring days when everything is perfect, and all five senses are on high alert. The air was sweet with the scent of the flowers growing by the stream's edge and scattered through the woods. Leaves rustled in the wind. The sun was warm, but not hot. The birds were singing. Fluffy white clouds dotted the sky. And the stream made beautiful music as it flowed over the rocks.

In Erda, water doesn't get polluted through manufacturing or sewer runoff. There is no plastic, and every container is biodegradable. In many ways, the dimension of Erda is perfect. The only thing that marred its perfection was Abbadon. But I had decided not to think about him for the rest of the day. There would be plenty of time to do so once we got to Kinver.

As we sat on rocks eating lunch, I finally got around to asking a question that had been rolling around in my head from the moment I came through the portal and a rock was right where I wanted to sit. It happened all the time. It had just happened. We were sitting on rocks that I hadn't noticed were there before we needed to rest. Then they somehow moved to where we could use them. I was learning that the trees were sentient beings. Were rocks?

The Priscillas were sunning themselves on a nearby rock when I asked the question.

"These rocks are here because we needed to sit on them, or in your case, lie on them, aren't they?" I asked.

"Did you just notice, or are you just getting around to asking the question?" La asked.

"Just getting around to the question."

"Okay. Then we have a question for you," La said, waving her free hand around to include her sisters, the other hand occupied with holding what looked like a chipmunk's tail. Was she trying to distract me? Where did that chipmunk come from, and why was she holding its tail?

When I realized that I was so distracted I couldn't remember what the question was in the first place, I dragged my attention back to La, trying to forget about the tail holding.

Finally, I couldn't hold it in any longer. "Why are you holding that chipmunk's tail, assuming it's a chipmunk?"

"Oh, it is," La laughed. "We're friends. Watch."

At which point, La jumped on the chipmunk's back and rode him up and down beside the stream. I couldn't help myself. I giggled. It was so zonking cute! When La got bored, or perhaps it was the chipmunk who got bored, she hopped off, kissed him on the nose, and settled back down beside her sisters on the rock.

"Good grief," I said. "Are you going to answer my question or not?"

"Which question is that?" La asked, acting all innocent.

I threw up my hands in exacerbation. "Rocks. Are they sentient?"

"And I ask you, Hannah aka Princess Kara Beth, did you or did you not just see me ride a chipmunk?"

"Did."

"So you accept that there are fairies riding chipmunks, a pileated dragon who is actually your friend Suzanne, trees that bend and move and know your thoughts, green blobs that shriek, and yet, you question if a rock is a sentient being?"

That was the most I had ever heard La talk. Ever. Being the youngest and smallest sister, I guess I had thought of her as a child. But what did I know of fairies? Or rocks?

"Stone people. They are called stone people," La continued. "They hold the records of the history of the planet, Gaia, in both Earth and Erda dimensions. Well, in all its dimensions because I am sure you know there are more.

"However, in Erda, as you know, we see these things where other dimensions may not. Like in the Earth Realm, where what you see and accept here is most often thought of as myth. In Erda we see, and honor, the intertwining of all life. We know that we are all One Life."

When the implications of what La had just said hit me, I jumped up off the rock. "I'm sitting on a person? A stone person? Is that okay with this rock or stone?"

"Hannah, you can be so ridiculous sometimes. Of course, you can. You climb trees. They love hosting you when you visit them that way. Rocks love providing you what you need too, even if it is just a place for you to sit," Pris said, standing there on her rock with her arms folded, tapping her feet, looking at me like I was an idiot.

Embarrassed, I lowered myself back down and patted the rock for good measure. "So, I could ask this rock anything about the history of Gaia, and it would answer me?"

"Of course. But you won't understand a word it says right now," Pris responded.

"Will I ever?" I asked.

"And that is a question I think we'll leave unanswered for now," Pris said, hopping up onto my shoulder. "We best be getting a move on if we want to reach Kinver before dark."

As we walked, I pondered the implications of what the Priscillas had told me. I was stepping on rocks. Rocks, trees, nature were all around me. I lived within it. If everything was speaking, then it was possible that someday I might hear what they were saying.

"Well, you hear me," Cahir said. "I believe you will hear what you need when it is time, Kara Beth."

I reached down and ran my hand through Cahir's fur, and silently thanked him. I swear I saw him give me the smallest of smiles.

I knew that I would look back on it and remember it as one of those perfect days that gets frozen in time. I will remember the feeling of the day. I will see myself with my hand on Cahir, and the Priscillas flitting around us, resting on me, and then skimming across the water, just dragging their toes in enough to make a trail. I would remember how Lady looked flying overhead, backlit by the sun, looking more like an angel than a dragon.

It was a perfect day. I knew it was probably going to be the last utterly perfect day for a long time.

ELEVEN

We reached the outskirts of Kinver at twilight, the time of transition. It seemed appropriate. I was transitioning between training alone to gathering a team to deal with Abbadon's latest horror creation.

I remembered the first time I saw Beru's village. It looked so quiet and peaceful, the perfect small town, and yet there had been two groups of people standing in the street arguing.

One group believed what Beru and Ruta had told them, that there was a monster named Abbadon who was bent on destroying all life. The other group thought it was fake news and were angry at Beru and Ruta for trying to scare them.

After Niko, my training instructor, told them what he had seen, and I had proved that I was their Princess Kara Beth by shooting lightning bolts from my hands, the village accepted that Beru had been telling the truth.

Five men from Kinver volunteered to come with us. Only four had returned. Perhaps it was a consolation to Kit's family that he had helped to stop the Shrieks and Shatterskin from destroying more towns and villages. I could only hope that was true.

One village Kit had helped save was his own. Kinver was still as charming as I remembered, a small town nestled in a valley, with gardens in every yard.

Last time we were here, the gardens were bare. Now, as I descended into the village, I could see flowers blooming, and

42

sprouts appearing in the vegetable gardens. Beru's people loved to garden, and the results were spectacular. Plus, what they did with the food they grew was mouthwatering.

Lady remained overhead, Cahir had already slipped into the fields, and the Priscillas had flown ahead. I thought that perhaps it was to let people know I was coming. So, I was alone as I walked the road into town.

The first person I saw was Liza, James' daughter. She was running full tilt down the road to me. I wanted to pick her up and spin her around, but in the short time since I had seen her, I swear she had grown six inches. Instead, I bent down and gathered her into my arms.

No words were needed. I was grateful for Liza's gift of the star necklace, and she was thankful that her father had returned safely. We unwound ourselves, each brushing tears away as if they never happened. Liza linked arms with me and chattered the whole way into town.

Yes, they knew I was coming. A big feast had been prepared. Yes, a few friends were waiting for me. Yes, she was happy that the star that showed me a 4D version of the world had been so helpful.

"Liza, do you want the star back? I can see it sometimes on my own," I said, when she mentioned the star.

We had almost reached the first home and people were starting to step out of their doors to wave at me.

"No. I don't need it anymore. And until I am old enough to travel with you, or that mean man is gone, you need it. It will show you what you need to know."

"It would be my honor, Liza. And someday we'll do a walkabout together, and you can show me the world as you see it."

"Yes!" Liza exclaimed, clapping her hands together, and then she grabbed my hands and started pulling me towards the town hall. "Come on. They are waiting for you!"

We started running together, saying hello to everyone in the streets, heading for who knows what. But with someone like Liza on our side I couldn't see how we could fail.

Well, I couldn't allow myself to see failure. As we ran, I promised myself once again that I would keep her and her people safe. Somehow.

I thought that I was prepared to see everyone, but when the door of the town hall opened, I almost fell to my knees in shock. Was everyone in the village here?

"Everyone except who is behind you," Liza said. It was only later that I realized that Liza had read my mind. I turned to see that all the people who had waved to us as we came through the streets were now standing behind us.

"How?" I asked.

"Berta and the Priscillas planned it, or at least they let us know you were coming so we could get ready," Liza whispered.

In the back of my mind, I realized that Berta and the Priscillas had probably been working together for a while. But at that moment all I could do was stand there in amazement. I wasn't even aware that tears were running down my face until Pris came over and dabbed my face with a cloth.

Standing in front of the group were the four men from Kinver who had traveled with us to defeat Shatterskin: James, his brother John, Thomas, and Mark. I ran to each of them preparing to shake hands, but instead was pulled into a hug by James, and then a group hug. They circled me as I sobbed. Once I recovered, I noticed that they each had an armband on that said "Kit." They had one for me, and I slipped it on.

"Come on, Hannah, let's celebrate. The village has been preparing this feast for days," James said, slipping one arm around my shoulders and holding Liza's hand with the other.

I smiled at James. He had remembered that I wanted a place where I could be just "Hannah," the girl I remembered being who had lived in the Earth dimension. I never wanted to lose that girl who loved unconditionally and knew the love of her family and friends.

James had promised me that Kinver would always be the place I could come to and not be royalty. He had told me I would always be like his daughter, and a father like James was just what I needed at that moment.

It took quite a while to get to the food because I insisted on stopping and thanking as many people as possible for their hospitality. I was aware that I hadn't protected Kit. I didn't get him home as I had promised, so their gratitude was almost too much for me.

Killing the Shrieks and Shatterskin had not made me feel bad. They weren't alive. They were machines driven by Abbadon. But Kit's death and one of the dragon's death had been weighing on me since the moment I had heard about them. I had to keep myself from saying, "If only," and letting that drag me down into one of my famous, but not loved, pity parties. It didn't stop me from having nightmares though.

Finally, Liza, tired of the constant hugging and shaking hands, grabbed me and said, "Come on, Hannah. I'm famished. Let's get food."

Something about her tone made me wonder what she was really up to, but I followed her through the crowd to the back of the room, wondering even more what was going on as the crowd kept stepping back to let us through.

I thought that I had done enough crying for the day, but when I saw who was standing there waiting for me, I couldn't help myself. I burst into tears and started running.

TWELVE

Standing there waiting for me as if it was the most natural thing in the world were the same two people who were waiting for me when I fell through the portal into Erda—Beru and Ruta. I hadn't known them then, but now I did. Knew them. Loved them.

Neither Ruta nor Beru were big huggers, but they both let me hold them so tight they probably couldn't breathe. In Beru's case, it was like hugging a flower, maybe a sweet pea. Her long arms circled me, and she laid her beautiful head on my shoulder for a minute. I could have stayed there forever. But I had to hug Ruta too. Hugging him was more like clutching a stump. Even so, his embrace as he patted me on my back made me weak with happiness.

After our hugs, we did our handshake—upside down, and finger wiggling. Beru loved doing that, and it made everyone laugh as Ruta did his best to finger wiggle back at us both.

"No questions right now, Kara Beth," Beru said, taking my arm and leading me to the food table. "Let's just celebrate with the village."

I nodded. I would have done anything Beru asked me to do at that moment. I suppose I should have known she would be there. After all, it was her village. But I hadn't dared to hope. It would have been too disappointing not to find her there when we arrived.

The party lasted for hours. Once again, Ruta, after drinking something that looked like syrup, got so happy he stood on the now empty food table and danced. But he wasn't alone. I got up, too, shocking myself. A few months before this would have been way too embarrassing. I was dancing with a tree stump—on a table. But Ruta's joy, as contained as he kept it, was so contagious, I couldn't help it.

It didn't matter, anyway. The entire village was dancing—children and adults. Even Mayor Tom joined Ruta and me on the table to dance.

Later, I realized that we danced that night because we needed to. We all knew that we were heading once again into a fight with Abbadon for the safety of everyone in the Kingdom of Zerenity. We had to take every minute of joy and celebration that we could, while it was there.

The moon was high in the sky when the party started to wind down, as parents took their children and headed home, stopping once again to thank us all for saving their village. We all nodded solemnly and did our best to look sure that we could do it again.

Finally, the room was empty except for me, Beru, Ruta, the Priscillas, and James. I was exhausted. We had traveled all day and danced all night.

I asked, "Are we leaving tonight?"

Beru looked at me like she often looked at me. As if I was an idiot. I loved it. I had missed that look. "Of course, we are not traveling tonight," she huffed, and then laughed.

We all laughed. I am sure it was one of those laughs that happen when you are so tired you can't see straight.

When he finally caught his breath, James said, "We prepared rooms for each of you, Hannah."

He wasn't kidding about preparing rooms. Mine was at his house. His wife, Lorraine, had left the party earlier, but was still waiting up and showed me to a room that reminded me of my bedroom back in Earth. The Priscillas stayed with me, but Beru took Ruta home to her house in the village.

Beru's parents had left the village at the first mention of Abbadon's movement east, and had gone to another town, leaving their home empty. It was a little surprising to me that Beru's parents hadn't returned yet, and I wondered how Beru felt about that.

However, the villagers had kept Beru's family home in good condition, or so she told me later, without mentioning how she felt about the fact that her parents hadn't returned home. Did she worry about them? Did she know where they were? None of my questions were answered that day.

I knew that Ruta's family had died in the same attack that my mother had died in. She had been visiting Ruta's village at the time. Visiting villages and towns was something that my mother loved to do, so I wasn't surprised to hear that was what she had been doing at the time of her death.

Ruta and I had never talked about it, but I know that when we had found the manufacturing plant where Abbadon was using his captives to run his machines, we had both hoped that we might discover his parents and my mother. When we didn't, we didn't say anything. What was there to say? It had been a small, impossible, hope for both of us.

We weren't the only ones who had lost loved ones. Someday I wanted to find every person who had lost someone and make sure that they were well, but that day would have to wait.

Breakfast at James' house was so wonderful I could almost pretend that it was just like breakfast back in the Earth Realm with my parents and my brother Ben, and sometimes all our friends. Except this breakfast was with a family that reminded me of flowers, someone who looked vaguely like a tree trunk, and fairies. It was fantastic.

We all helped Lorraine clean up afterward. I knew what we were doing. We were being both helpful and delaying the inevitable. We had a job to do. I wasn't sure how long the walk was to the

Castle, but I was sure that Beru and Ruta were going to want to get moving. However, they didn't seem to be in a big hurry, lingering over their drinks and chatting with Liza about what she was studying in school.

Finally, I couldn't take it anymore. We had never started walking later than sunrise, and now it was mid-morning. "What the ziffer?" I asked. "Why aren't we getting going?"

Ruta grunted. I loved it. He was back to being the Ruta I remembered. The Priscillas giggled, and Beru just gave me one of her famous looks that I had seen scare grown men. Ah, back to normal.

No one said anything. Finally, Liza took pity on me and whispered that they had another surprise for me.

Zut, another surprise? Was it a person? When I heard the low sound of a gathering of notes, I knew what it was. As the song became louder, I rushed outside.

I could see the Sound Bubble was on its way, and there was someone inside it.

THIRTEEN

The Sound Bubble landed, and Zeid stepped out. I was torn between being mad at him for leaving me with just a note saying he would see me soon, or the joy of seeing his face again. He smiled at me, and I forgot about being mad. I apparently also forgot about being a Princess because I almost knocked him over as I ran to meet him.

For a moment I was worried. What if Zeid didn't like me anymore? It wasn't an idle worry, because even though I remembered that we were to be married one day, I couldn't remember if we chose or if it was chosen for us. However, at that moment it didn't matter. I was just happy to see him. Truthfully, it probably never mattered, because even when I couldn't remember a thing about my life in Erda, my heart did little flutters from the moment I saw him.

The only thing that had stopped me from revealing my feelings before had been Johnny's friendship bracelet that I had been wearing. I glanced at my wrist. It wasn't there anymore. I had returned it to Johnny before going to Eiddwen. Suzanne had taken it back through the portal to the Earth dimension. But since she hadn't talked to me since she returned, I had no idea how Johnny had felt about it.

Now, I only had the bracelet with the picture-jasper stone on my wrist. The one Professor Link had given to me, or as he said, returned to me. It felt familiar, although I still didn't know why. Did it have a power I was supposed to know how to use?

All that went through my head as I ran toward Zeid. One question was answered when he picked me up and swung me around in a circle. I'm not little, but Zeid managed it somehow. The hug he gave me afterward alleviated my fear that he didn't care about me anymore.

"So you missed me," he said.

"Maybe," I said.

"Don't you want to know where I've been, and where we are going?" Zeid asked.

"Maybe," I answered

'Oh, for Zut's sake," Pris said, flying at us both. I ducked. I knew she was heading for pulling my hair. Missing me, she got Zeid's hair instead. She pulled at the lock of dark hair that kept falling over his forehead until he said, "Ow," which struck everyone, including me, as hilarious.

With Pris around, no one could take themselves too seriously. Pris' sisters had no problem ingratiating themselves with Zeid. After a few quick kisses on his cheek, they returned to my shoulder and stared at him. Not that I could blame them. Zeid is easy to look at. But he looked tired in spite of his trying to look as if he wasn't.

When he saw me looking at him with concern, he shook his head slightly as if to tell me not to ask, and turned to the rest of the group standing there, and said, "Are you all ready?"

"Do you want something to eat first?" Lorraine asked.

Zeid took both her hands in his and said, "Thank you, Lorraine, but I think we best be leaving."

It wasn't until I saw the tears in Lorraine's eyes that I realized what was happening. All four men who had fought with us before were coming with us again.

"Oh, no! I can't take you away from your families again. Liza needs you, James. The village needs all of you. I can't. No," I shouted.

I even stamped my foot, which I'm sure looked absurd. I didn't know what else to do. I couldn't be responsible for their deaths. I wanted to come back to Kinver and be Hannah again someday, and I needed these people to be there when I did.

It was Liza and her father who calmed me down, at least enough to grudgingly admit that it was their choice. Liza said she and her mother would be fine. The rest of the village would watch over them. James explained that he had to go. He wouldn't be able to live with himself if he didn't help us. The other three men nodded in agreement.

"Besides, you need me to question everything don't you?" John said.

It was true, John did question everything and that was a good thing even though sometimes we didn't like it. Thomas and Mark said they were going for Kit. He gave his life to save the Kingdom. They weren't going to let him down now, and that was all there was to it.

Once I realized I couldn't stop them from coming, I told them how grateful I was, and I meant it. But then I realized how many of us there were.

"Are we all going in the Sound Bubble?" I asked.

While we had been talking, it was sitting there silently, shimmering in the sun. Before, the bubbles had dissolved when they landed. This one appeared to be waiting for us. But there were so many of us.

"And what about Cahir and Lady? And although I love riding in that thing, I thought we weren't to use it unless it was an emergency. Wait. Is this an emergency? And are we going to the Castle? Wait. Where are we going?" I sputtered the last of the questions.

"Geez, Kara Beth. Questions, questions, get a grip," Zeid said, turning to look where Lady had landed on the ground near the bubble. "I'll let Suzanne answer you."

As if it was something she did every day while we watched, Lady morphed into Suzanne. Once again, I wasn't sure if I should be angry or happy, but I chose happy and rushed over to hug her. I had even more questions, but at least I knew enough to wait to ask those.

"Here are your answers, Kara. Yes, it is somewhat of an emergency. At least we don't want to take the few days it would to walk to the Castle. So, yes, we are going to the Castle. Yes, we are all going in a Sound Bubble, except Cahir who refuses and has already started across country to get there."

I started to ask another question, and she held up her finger to stop me. "No, we can't all fit into the bubble. There are two."

Across the valley, I heard the harmony of a hundred notes as a second bubble arrived. The bubbles hovered over our groups and then settled around us. I loved the feeling inside the Sound Bubble. I knew that Ruta didn't like heights, so I pretended that I needed to hold on to him as ours rose into the air. He probably knew what I was doing, but he let me, and I hoped it helped.

I waved to the village of Kinver and whispered that I would be back, and prayed that I was telling the truth.

FOURTEEN

The first time I arrived at the Castle, people were standing outside waiting for us. Unhappy people. Angry people. Unhappy and mad at me because they thought I had deserted them. They bowed and glared at the same time. Having lost my memory of the me that had come from Erda, I had no idea why they were mad, or why they were bowing.

Suzanne had been with me then, too, and she had pinched and pulled me to direct my bowing and walking. I had been blown away by the Castle and beings of all kinds waiting for me as if I was royalty. Even though, for some reason, they were not happy about it.

It turned out I am royalty. But as soon as I could, I put a stop to the practice of bowing. I am just like everyone else. It was only an accident of birth that I am a princess. But since I am, I can choose how I'm treated.

And now, most of the people of my father's Kingdom of Zerenity have learned that I was sent to the Earth dimension to keep me safe. In retrospect, it had been both dumb and cruel. Royalty could send their child away, but everyone else had to hope that Abbadon would not target their village and their children. They felt it wasn't fair, and it wasn't.

If people were waiting outside for us this time, I didn't see them because instead of landing outside the Castle, we slipped through the open roof of the atrium. That was a surprise to me. I had no idea that the atrium roof opened.

This time the people waiting for us were people I knew—every single zonking one of them. Even the metal toadstools were there. And if metal toadstools could look happy, they did. That meant there must be food, but at that moment I didn't care. I looked at all those people, and I couldn't believe how happy I felt.

Even Pita and his brothers were there. I didn't think that Teddy the Whistle Pig would be at the Castle since his home was underground, but I saw Teddy standing at the edge of the crowd, looking like a huge bear.

It was Teddy that yelled, "Pumpkin toes!" as the bubble dissolved around me. I love the silly names he makes up for me, and I wish I were clever enough to make some up for him. But instead, I let myself be wrapped up in his big bear arms.

In spite of the danger I could feel all around the Castle, inside there was celebration. A beautiful spread of food was ready for us. Little name tags told us where to sit. At the head of the table was Earl, otherwise known as Coro, the commander of the storms. His wife, Ariel, sat next to him. She ruled the wind. I could see the two of them holding hands beneath the table, which made me love Earl even more, even though he scared the ziffer out of me when he raised his voice. Seriously, even the trees trembled when Earl spoke.

It was a huge table, and yet somehow we could hear each other. The roof of the atrium had closed, but since it was a clear roof we could still see the sky, and the atrium overflowed with trees and flowers. It was a magical space.

Zeid and Beru sat beside me. The Priscillas hovered everywhere. They flew from shoulder to shoulder, sometimes bestowing kisses.

Ruta claimed to dislike their attention, but I knew it wasn't true. I had learned to see the smile he tried to hide. When Ruta laughed, he sounded like a garbage can lid rattling, or a frog croaking depending on what he was laughing about. But Ruta's smile was soft and sweet, even though it was rare. He sat beside Beru with the Ginete on his left.

All of my teachers were there. Niko, who led our team and tried to teach me how to fight and defend myself even though I knew he thought of me as clumsy. He is right about that.

Aki sat with him. I used to call her Miss Floaty before I knew her name because she floated instead of walking most of the time. Aki was in charge of my flexibility and meditation practice. She was also the one who had told me the story of the two brothers in the metal space ship shaped like a snake that had seeded the two dimensions and started this whole thing. I needed to talk to her more about that.

Professor Link, the man I called Pinhead until I knew his real name, was beside Aki. Now that I knew that they could all read my mind, I realized that they all knew the names I used to call them. I flushed thinking how rude I had been. They all smiled at me.

Zut, they were reading my mind again. I realized I didn't care. It was Link who kept us all in contact all the time. I had missed his voice in my head, and his attempt to help me remember my magic skills. Now that he was back in my head, I couldn't have been happier.

My teachers. I hoped that the practice I had done without them would make them proud of me, but I knew that desire was something I had to squash before they discovered it. They would not let me live it down. Still, I did harbor a hope that what I had done would please them. Maybe that need would never go away, and I would have to live with it.

Across from me sat Leif and Sarah. I was surprised because I had never seen them at the Castle before. I knew them both from the Earth dimension, and now they lived in this one. Or was it the other way around? It always confused me.

I thought that Leif and Sarah were first from Erda and then went to Earth and then returned, but I wasn't sure. I did know that

Suzanne was first from Erda and traveled back and forth between the dimensions as a bridge between the two Realms.

Suzanne had told me that Earl and Ariel had lived in the Earth dimension to bring together some people in Earth who needed to meet. We called them the Stone Circle. Johnny was a member of the Stone Circle. But then Sarah and Leif had been members of that circle too, and now they were here. See? Confusing.

What made some of this possible was the fact that Earth time and Erda time move differently. So, although Leif and Sarah were in the Earth dimension a long span of time for Earth time, in Erda time they hadn't been gone long at all. Once I started thinking about the whole dimension and time travel thing, it confused me.

It was Sarah who answered my unspoken question, "We started here, Kara Beth, just like you. We left before you did out of a desire to learn more about the Earth dimension. We hoped to impact it in a good way and to enlarge our understanding of life. What we didn't know was that we would forget where we had come from, just as you forgot."

"When Leif returned with Suzanne's help, he began to remember. When he came to visit me in the Earth dimension, he started to tell me about who we were here. So before I returned to Erda, I had remembered who I had been here."

"It's a good thing, too," Aki piped in. "Sarah, as the Oracle, was able to help you remember sooner, which made it possible to defeat the Shrieks and Shatterskin."

"So while you were gone, there wasn't an Oracle here?" I asked.

"Until Abbadon decided he wanted to rule the planet, there wasn't a need for me. We all thought it was safe for us to visit the Earth dimension," Sarah answered.

"And then it wasn't," I whispered.

"And then it wasn't," Sarah agreed.

FIFTEEN

I thought we would have our meeting right after dinner, but I was wrong. Earl took charge and said that everyone needed a good night's sleep before we began our talks about how to defeat Abbadon's latest weapon. So far, I hadn't heard anything about it. I didn't have its name, and I didn't know what it did. I knew nothing about how far away it was or what was going to be required of us.

When I tried to ask someone, they would shush me. I hate being shushed. That's why I think Beru and Ruta especially love to do it. They like to see my reaction.

The Priscillas always pretend that they don't know anything, but I was discovering that it was almost always a lie. The fact that they had been speaking to Berta when I thought no one was paying any attention to me proved my point. But I was proving it only to myself because no one was listening. They were too busy shushing me and enjoying each other.

I finally gave in to enjoying dinner and stopped trying to get answers to my questions. It would have been stupid not to. The food was incredible and diverse. I knew so little about how food arrived on the table, that the possibility that it was produced magically crossed my mind. Perhaps there was a species of beings that only prepared food, and I hadn't met them yet. My mind drifted away to imagine what they might look like and how they cooked, not noticing that everyone was staring at me. When I broke out of the daydream and brought my attention back to the table, everyone started laughing.

Ziffer. They were all watching my daydream. I wanted to huff at them and tell them to get out of my head, but then I realized how much I had missed them not being in my head and I started laughing with them. When the metal toadstools started doing a version of a laugh—think of shaking a can filled with stones because that's what it sounded like—I could barely control myself.

"Do you like that?" Teddy asked, referring to the toadstools laughter.

Wiping my eyes as the tears ran down my face from laughing so hard, I nodded. "Did you program that?"

"I got bored," Teddy responded, which prompted another round of laughter.

After dinner, Zeid took my hand and said he would see me in the morning. I was disappointed. I had hoped to spend some private time with him. I had questions to ask him and feelings that wanted to pop out and express themselves.

"We have to wait, Kara," Zeid said as he tucked a strand of hair behind my ear.

"It's childish for me to ask why, isn't it?" I said.

Zeid looked at me with such a sad expression that I knew it wasn't easy for him, either.

I leaned in and kissed him on the cheek. And for a brief moment, I felt his arms go around me. It wasn't nearly enough, and it didn't answer any questions other than that we were in this together. Whatever "this" was.

"I'm walking you to your room," Beru said, dragging me back to the present.

"Just like old times," I answered. "Only this time I know where we are going, and how to find my room."

"And this time, I am not going to lock the door," Beru laughed.

"I know why you aren't," I replied. "But I still don't know why you did."

We both laughed. Beru wasn't going to lock me in because she knew I had figured out how to unlock doors, all doors, anywhere. But I still didn't understand why she had locked the door in the first place. Then it dawned on me. Perhaps it was so I would practice unlocking them.

By then, I was in my room. Beru gave me a look, turned and left the room, and then locked the door behind her. "Real funny, Beru," I called out and with a flick of my wrist, unlocked the door.

I swear I heard Beru say, "That's my girl," but it was probably only wishful thinking.

Aki came for me in the morning. Not the way most people do, of course. She didn't knock on my door, or shake me as I lay in bed, or even sit in a chair waiting for me to wake up. No, Aki was hanging in the air, eyes closed, lying on her side, with one arm under her head and another hanging down into space. I had seen her do that before and I knew that there was a ledge of some sort she was lying on that was invisible. But still, it was quite disconcerting.

Besides, the last time she had been waiting for me to wake up was after I had been injured during the attack on Shatterskin. I felt a frisson of fear seeing her lying there again.

I was instantly awake. "Is there something wrong?" I croaked, not having used my voice yet that morning.

Aki yawned, stretched like only a goddess of some kind could look stretching, and said, "No, just thought it would be lovely to have a little chat before meeting everyone else."

Aki slipped off the invisible edge and stood by my bed. As much as I tried to deny it, I was a teeny, tiny, bit jealous of Aki. To start with, Aki was so beautiful it was hard to wrap my head around it. Ethereal wasn't quite the word because she was also so grounded. That didn't take into account what she could do, like hang in the air, and float across the floor.

The first time I saw Aki I wondered if the form that I saw her in was her true form. Standing by my bed, Aki's pale blue eyes glowed in the half-light coming through the curtain. She smiled at me, and they turned dark blue. I almost had the feeling that Aki could twist herself around and turn into a wisp of smoke, or slither across the floor without making a sound.

Aki flicked her long pale white hair into the air, and for a moment she hung there just like a wisp of smoke. And then she was gone. In my head, I heard her say, "Meet me in the training room, little one."

Back to "little one" again. I didn't mind. Anyone who could turn herself into a wisp of smoke just because I imagined that she could had the right to call me 'little one' anytime she wished.

As I pulled on my clean leggings and tunic—one of the many benefits of being in the Castle again was clean clothes every morning that I had nothing to do with making clear—I wondered if the second half of what I was thinking was also right.

I thought about the story Aki had told me of the two brothers traveling in the snake-shaped space ship through the universe for thousands and thousands of years.

How old is Aki anyway? I wondered. And was she one of the people on that ship, or one of their descendants? Besides, I still didn't know if it was a true story or not.

"True enough," was the answer I heard.

SIXTEEN

If I had thought I was going to the training room to have tea with Aki as we sometimes did, I was utterly mistaken. There was no chatting involved at all. Instead, Aki ran me through the most intense flow training I had ever experienced.

From the moment I walked through the door, she had me going. At the end I was breathing so hard I thought I would pass out. Then she told me to sit, meditate, and intentionally bring my heart rate down and slow my breathing so that by the time we finished I was taking only a few breaths a minute.

"Could be a little better, Kara," she said, indicating that the lesson was over. "But on the other hand, it's better than I expected."

There was no time to reply to her comment because Beru was at the door. Beru didn't speak. She didn't say anything about my slow walking or drained face. Instead, she took me straight to Niko, who was waiting in the outside training space. All I could think was, "Oh, no!"

Niko turned to me, and I knew I was a goner. He started commanding, and I had no choice but to do what he said. Jump, kick, dodge, get out of the way, get in the way, throw lightning at a target, and spin in the air, fly to the tree and back, over and over again.

After what felt like a hundred hours, Niko raised his hand and motioned for me to sit down. I tried to sit but ended up falling on my butt. "An elephant could sit more gracefully than that, Kara Beth," Niko said.

"I couldn't agree with you more," I muttered, as I tried to sit upright but kept tilting to the side with my legs sprawled out in front of me.

When I realized that Niko had left the practice space, I lay back down and stared at the sky, too tired to try and figure out what had just happened. No wonder they had fed me so well the night before. At first, I had been upset that I hadn't had any breakfast yet, but at that moment I was glad. It would have never stayed down.

"So what if I was an enemy right now?" I heard. "Could you get up and fight me?"

Lifting my head enough to see who was talking, I saw Leif standing in front of me holding a staff. Not like the ones that we used for fighting, although I supposed he could use it for that. It was much fancier.

"No," I answered truthfully. "And that's a cool staff, Leif. Never saw you with that before."

Leif looked at the staff in his hand and smiled. "It is, isn't it? I've had it for a long time. And right now, you need to try and take it from me."

I started giggling. "That's funny, Leif," I said, lowering myself back down to the ground with a groan. "But I am too pooped to play right now."

"Who said we were playing, Princess!" Leif said in a voice I had never heard before.

A split second later, I felt the ground shake, and a bolt of lightning streaked down from the sky just missing my outstretched arm.

I screamed, "What the ziffer!" as I rolled away from the lightning blast. The sky had grown dark, and I could barely see Leif encased within a blue haze. I had seen the blue haze before, but it had felt warm and soothing. I could scarcely comprehend that Leif had been that soothing blue haze because the man I knew as Leif was standing in front of me, holding a golden staff high into the air. He wasn't looking warm and soothing at all. I had never seen anyone look so terrifying.

"Again, Princess?" Leif yelled, striking the staff once again into the ground.

This time I expected the lightning and rolled closer to Leif, hoping he wasn't planning on striking himself. It worked. The bolt landed yards away from me. But if Leif thought I could take his staff away from him, he was mistaken. Even if I had any energy left to fight him, I had no idea how to do it.

"What do you have, Kara?" I heard Professor Link ask.

"Nothing, nothing," I answered as I rolled again, watching Leif's staff come down.

"You have us. Ask for help," I heard. "Help," I squeaked, as the lightning missed me by a fraction of a second, and the ground shook, and the sky grew darker, ready to split open again.

Then I realized I had something else. First, I knew that Leif would never hurt me. Then, I remembered when the Priscillas and I were inside of Shatterskin trying to destroy something we had already destroyed. We won by recognizing that we were looking at an illusion. Was this another illusion?

Thinking of the wise and gentle Leif that I knew, I shouted at Leif, "This is not you!"

Within seconds the dark skies, the blue haze, the lightning disappeared, and Leif was standing before me with one of his rare, but beautiful, smiles.

I looked around the practice yard and saw everyone else was there, too. Everyone. Standing around us. Waiting. Nothing had changed. There was no place where lightning had struck. No shattering of the ground. It had been an illusion.

I staggered to my feet and started swearing every Erda swear word I knew, vaguely remembering I still did not know why every curse word in Erda began with a z.

"What the zonking, ziffering, zonking, zut was that?" I yelled. It wasn't a loud yell. I was still shaking, and my voice matched my insides.

I turned the most withering look I had onto Zeid, who was standing there casually with the Priscillas on his shoulder. He narrowed his azure eyes at me and smiled.

"What right do you have ...," I started to say, but then everything started turning black, and I heard someone say, "I've got you, Princess," and everything went dark.

SEVENTEEN

"**Y**ou fainted," Beru said.

"Really? I wondered what that was," I said with as much sarcasm as I could muster, lying flat on my back in the dirt. It was just the two of us. If I didn't feel so zonking awful I would have thought the entire morning was just a bad dream.

"No need to get all snotty about it, Miss Kara," Beru snipped right back. "I didn't do anything."

"You didn't do anything?" I huffed as I attempted to sit up. "Who brought me to all these ass-kicking training sessions this morning? Don't try and tell me you didn't know about it.

"To think I used to think you were part of some fairy-like race. I think you are really part of a medieval torture crew, you cow, you!"

Beru stepped back. "Well, for one thing, the Priscillas are the fairies, and you know that, and for another, I don't know what medieval torture is unless it is putting up with you taking things out on me, and being an ungrateful brat!"

I was getting ready to respond when I heard, "Hey, hey, hey. What's going on, Bunny Hops, and Miss Beru?"

At the sound of Teddy's voice, I broke down. "What's wrong with me?" I said as he gathered me into his arms. "How could I talk to Beru like that?"

I looked over at her and was shocked to see that Beru was crying too.

"I'm so sorry, Beru. I didn't mean a thing I said."

Beru nodded at me and smiled. But I could tell she was hurt, and it would take a while to regain her confidence. I wasn't kidding when I asked what was wrong with me. It felt like some strange thought-worm was in my head for a minute, making me feel as if hurting Beru was okay because she deserved it.

"Beru knows what happened, don't you Beru?" Teddy said, reaching for Beru's hand while holding me close to him. Beru hesitated, but let him touch her and gather her into his side.

"Come on," Teddy said, walking us towards the door into the Castle. "Let's get some food and drink into you, Kara, and maybe a bit of a rest, and then we'll talk about it."

It was Teddy who took me to my room, where a side table of food was waiting for me. Beru had begged off saying she had to take care of something, but her face gave her away. Maybe she understood what had happened, but it didn't change the fact that I had hurt her feelings. Beru, who could face Abbadon's monsters, was hurt by my words. I wasn't sure what I was going to do.

"What did you mean when you said that Beru knows what's going on, Teddy? We've teased each other before, but this was different. I didn't feel like myself at all. What is happening?"

"Think about what it felt like, Kara. You are going to need that information. Eat now. Get some rest. Aki will come to collect you in a bit. I'll talk to Beru and make sure she's okay."

"Thank you, Teddy," I said and leaned back onto the bed. The food would have to wait. Rest first.

Aki didn't have to wake me. I woke up ravenous and had just finished devouring everything on my plate when Aki popped her head in the door and asked me if I was ready.

I had so many questions to ask that I didn't ask any. What was the point? Aki didn't volunteer any either. Just before we reached the meeting room, Aki touched my arm and smiled at me. It was hard not to smile back at her, so we were both smiling when we entered the room filled with everyone who looked relieved that I was smiling.

"Well played, Aki," I pushed into her mind.

"I thought you would like them to know that you are ready, Kara Beth," Aki answered.

She was right. Whatever had happened that morning was for my benefit. Not to hurt me, but to show me something. They would be worried about my reaction. A smile was the perfect way to let them know that I understood. Not that I understood anything except that it had been part of my training for whatever we were going to face next.

Leif took my arm and led me to a seat beside him. His staff was leaning against the wall in the corner. It was looking innocent, if an inanimate object can look innocent.

I heard someone ask, "Who says it's inanimate?"

I wasn't sure who asked the question, but it was true. Who said it was inanimate? One thing I was learning was that nothing is inanimate.

I looked around the table. I expected everyone to be there, but the Ginete, Teddy, Earl, Ariel, and the men from the village were missing.

"Is this a planning meeting? Why isn't everyone here?" I asked Leif.

"They are busy doing other things right now. This meeting is for you, Kara," Suzanne said. "This meeting is to bring you up to date with Abbadon's latest weapon."

"Does it have a name yet?" I asked.

"It does," Suzanne answered. "Its name is Deadsweep."

"Because it leaves everything it touches dead?" I asked, thinking of the Shrieks and Shatterskin.

"It does. But it doesn't work at all like the Shrieks or Shatterskin. They were crude killing machines. The Deadsweep is much more subtle and effective."

The blood drained from my face, and I could see that my hands had turned white. I couldn't see how anything could be more effective than Abbadon's last monsters. No, they weren't subtle. They were loud. They announced themselves. But to me, they had seemed to be very efficient killing machines.

"How?"

"After you fainted, what happened?" Aki asked.

"I woke up."

"And did what?"

Now I flushed. They knew that I had been rude to Beru. How did they know?

"I treated Beru as if she was my enemy," I whispered, so embarrassed I wanted to run out of the room.

"Imagine that feeling one hundred times worse. What might you have done?" Niko asked.

I looked around the room. Everyone was still waiting for my answer. Whatever I said, it would have to be true because my friends were trying to tell me something.

"I think if that feeling was a hundred times worse, I might have tried to kill her."

The room was still. It was as if a deadly secret was hanging in the air, and speaking it would bring it to light.

When no one spoke, I asked, "Does this have something to do with what you are calling the Deadsweep?"

Leif put his hand on my hand and said, "I am afraid it does, Kara. I am sorry that we had to show you that way, but you needed to experience it for yourself."

"It was like something else was thinking for me and making me feel that way," I said.

It was Beru who whispered it. "That is the Deadsweep."

EIGHTEEN

"Okay," I said, trying to keep things as light as possible despite what I had just heard. "You are telling me some kind of thought-worm got into my head and made me act that way? And you are calling it the Deadsweep?

"There are just too many weird things about that. How could it get in my head? Why? This is Abbadon doing it? I don't get it," I finished. I was utterly frustrated and frightened at the same time.

"Those are all great questions, Kara," Leif said. "We don't have all the answers yet. It's one reason we kept you away for the last few months, to keep you safe from what you are calling the thought-worm, because we are not sure how people are getting infected with it."

"Wait, that's why you kept me away? I thought it was for me to learn to train by myself. And how could I have been safe? I was all by myself." I paused, remembering that the Priscillas knew Berta, and Lady were always flying above me. "Was I all by myself?"

"Good lord, sometimes you can be dense," Pris said, pulling my hair. "Of course you weren't. And yes, you were supposed to be training by yourself instead of waiting for other people to show you things."

"Did a pretty good job of it too," Niko said, and Aki nodded in agreement.

That took me by surprise. I felt myself tear up again. After that morning's training session, I thought I had been a complete failure.

"No, you would have never made it through the morning if you hadn't done well training by yourself the last few months," Suzanne added, seeing my reaction.

"As for being by yourself, are you serious?" Beru added. She might have understood what had happened in the training area that morning better than I did, but I could tell she was still upset with me. This thought-worm thing was scary. Even though I hadn't meant to hurt her, I had damaged our friendship.

"Do you think we would have left the village of Eiddwen, with your father, the King, and you, the future queen in it, unprotected? Ever?"

I silently shook my head, ashamed for not knowing. Ashamed for not being aware enough, or doubting my friends.

No one spoke, letting the silence gather, waiting for me to snap out of it. I could feel what Beru called my pity party coming on. In so many ways I wanted to just put my head down on the table and go back to sleep. Let someone else be Princess. I was too stupid to be a ruler.

Pris pulled my hair. "Cut it out!" she yelled as loud as she could.

"Kara Beth, that thought process that takes you down doesn't feel dangerous to you, but it is," Sarah said. "It's almost as dangerous as the evil thoughts you had this morning towards Beru."

Everyone nodded, and Aki took over. "If we are going to win this battle, defeat the Deadsweep, then the first thing to be aware of is what you are thinking—more than you have ever done before. None of us can let ourselves sink into depression, or despair, or the idea that we can't do something or we aren't good enough. It's opening the door to what Abbadon is doing with Deadsweep.

"We've talked about this so many times, Kara. What door, what channels do you have open to others? You have to monitor what you are listening to and communicating at all times. There isn't any room for self-doubt. You, we, can't afford it.

"This affects all of us. We are all susceptible to these kinds of suggestions. That's why, once again, we have to do this together. We have to watch each other for signs of infection."

I nodded, letting Sarah know that I had heard her, and then asked Leif, "So Abbadon planted that suggestion in my head this morning? The one where I was furious with Beru for no reason?"

"No, we did," Niko answered. "First, we had to get you so exhausted you weren't paying attention, and then we planted the suggestion in your head that Beru was your enemy. Beru knew what we were doing. She agreed to it."

Niko broke off and looked over at Beru before continuing, "And despite that, she reacted, even though she was fully aware that you didn't know what had happened. You can see how dangerous this would be if it were worse, and people didn't know what was happening to them."

"What about the scary thing Leif did? Was that part of the suggestion?" I asked.

Leif answered this time, "Yes. We wanted you to use the ability to see the illusion and call it. You know me. You know I would never hurt you, so you were able to see through the hypnotic suggestion that I wanted to kill you.

"However, it works the other way around too. Evil can masquerade as friendship producing the illusion that you are safe when you are in danger."

What Leif was saying was scaring me. The implications were staggering.

"We have been monitoring the increased levels of violence that are being recorded around the Kingdom. We had thought that it was the residual sound waves from the Shrieks that was causing it. People acting out. Fighting between neighbors.

"But even though there are no more Shrieks, these outbreaks are occurring more and more. We have never had a problem with violence of any kind, so not only is it terrifying that it's happening, but no one knows how to respond."

I thought about the police force in Kinver where before Abbadon, the biggest problem they had was animals stuck in trees. That level of peace and harmony had existed throughout the entire Kingdom of Zerenity. Now that their peace was being disturbed by their own people, I could see how dealing with it would be overwhelming.

"It's like a disease that is sweeping through towns. But there is no way to know when someone has been infected with it until they act out. They don't look like anything is wrong. They could be your friend or neighbor and then one minute they are not. They become an enemy bent on destroying. We've even had incidents of people killing each other," Suzanne said.

Now I understood the fear I felt.

"There is no way to know?" I whispered.

"Not that we have found. Yet. That's what we have been working on."

Aki spoke up. "We think that the person gets taken over. But what we don't know is if they are gone forever, or temporarily. They are like what the Native Americans in the Earth Realm called Skin Walkers. People are walking around in their skins, but not the people you know."

I thought of all the movies I had seen about Zombies or the movie Body Snatchers.

"More like body snatchers,' Professor Link said, reading my mind. "They don't look scary. They seem like the same person. They aren't weird beings walking around with half their face falling off. Nothing has changed, except for something that will trigger them into violence.

"We have to find how they are being infected and stop that. And we have to turn off the trigger. Otherwise, we have people acting like suicide bombers walking among us, ready to destroy everything. Which is how we know this is Abbadon's doing. It's his goal. Win at all costs, including destroying everything that lives."

NINETEEN

When Leif stood up, we all understood that the meeting was over. I didn't know what to do. Everything I had heard made it seem as if we were up against impossible odds. However, I knew I couldn't let the news lead me back into depression or helplessness. But I could feel the urge to give in beating against the walls of my mind, trying to take over.

No one said anything as they left the room. What was there to say? Leif gestured for me to stay, so I remained seated. He waited until everyone was gone, then sat back down and swiveled in his chair to look at me.

Leif in Erda looked almost like the Leif in the Earth dimension. It made sense because they were the same man. Aki had explained to me that not every dimension had a version of ourselves in them. Sometimes we were the only one. Like Suzanne, Leif, Sarah, and me. Maybe more of the people I knew were only found in Erda, but so far, we were the ones I knew about.

On the other hand, other versions of ourselves could be in dimensions no one had visited yet. There are so many dimensions it is probably impossible to know. Besides, I hadn't met anyone who had traveled to more than Earth and Erda. However, I understood that there were people in Erda who had traveled extensively. I wondered who they were and if I would ever get to meet them.

The difference was that in Erda, everything about Leif was a bit more vivid—his hair whiter and his eyes bluer. If Leif wasn't smiling and you didn't know him, you might think he was angry because his look was so focused.

But as far as I knew, Leif rarely got angry. Instead, he got more focused. That morning's encounter showed his ability to direct his energy to where he wanted it to go. It also made me think that I hardly knew Leif—at least how he existed in Erda.

He wasn't smiling when he swiveled in his chair to look at me. I was glad that I knew him well enough to know that look just meant he was focused, not angry. I don't know why it took me so long to notice what Leif had reminded me of all along. The clue was probably that innocent-looking staff waiting in the corner of the room.

One of my biggest problems is saying what comes to mind without filtering it first. So without thinking, I said, "Zut, Leif, are you a wizard? Like the ones in fairy tales, or in Harry Potter books?"

As soon as the words were out of my mouth, I wondered if it was a wise thing to ask someone if they were a wizard. Was it against the rules? Rude? Stupid?

"None of those things, Hannah," Leif said, resorting to my Earth name. Since I knew that Leif never said or did anything without a reason behind it, I thought that he was reminding me I already knew him. There was nothing to fear from the Earth Leif, so, therefore, there was nothing to fear from the Erda Leif.

When Leif smiled at me, I knew I was on track. That was reassuring.

"But you still want an answer, don't you?" Leif said.

I nodded, all the thoughts of Deadsweep temporarily gone from my head.

"I guess I look like a wizard, don't I?" Leif asked.

I waited.

"Well," he sighed. "I suppose I am. However, even I am not sure all of what being a wizard means—still working that out. Just like you are working out what a princess is, and what a princess does. Perhaps we get to choose the role that we play inside this story in Erda, Kara Beth.

"For now, there is something you must do. It's the most important thing all of us need to do. Repair any rifts in our lives. And for you, right now that is working out what is going on between you and your friend Beru. Instead of the physical riff where we went to find the Shrieks and Shatterskin, we have to find the mental and emotional rifts within ourselves and with our friends, and close them up. Heal them.

"It is those rifts that Abbadon will target. It's how an infection like Deadsweep might be able to get in. Just like infections can get in through cuts in the skin. They need to be healed.

"Deadsweep is a mental infection. At the moment, it's an invisible infection, which makes it more dangerous than the Shrieks or Shatterskin. Therefore, we can't take any chances. Repair the riffs. No matter how small.

"The one that is right in front of you is the one with Beru. It's dangerous for you both, and then ultimately for all of us. See if you can discover why her feelings are so hurt. That's something you can do right now."

I nodded and then impulsively leaned over and kissed his cheek. Leif smiled, his blue eyes twinkling back at me. At that moment, all was right with the world. Leif patted my hand and said, "You have it in you to be a great queen, Princess Kara Beth."

Stunned, I watched him as he stood—almost like water standing up—it was so smooth, and reached out his hand for his staff. Before I could blink, the staff was in his hand, looking ordinary even though I knew it wasn't. As Leif walked out the door, he turned once more and smiled at me.

I stood and looked down the hallway after him, wondering at what I had just seen. I didn't see what I now knew to be a wizard. Instead, I saw a blue haze surrounding a blue light—Leif and Sarah.

There was so much I didn't know. And I knew there was not that much time to learn it.

TWENTY

I went looking for Beru. That she wasn't waiting for me
reinforced what Leif had told me. We had a problem. Beru
always waited for me. She had been my guide from the moment
I fell through the portal.

Ruta, on the other hand, hadn't been particularly happy about
my arrival. Truthfully, he had been a huge grouch head. However,
Beru took on my clumsiness, confusion, and lack of awareness, as
if it was a pleasure to help me.

It was Beru who taught me how to feel in order to see things that
are invisible to the eye. I first learned to do that by internally feeling
to find the door to get to my room in the Castle. After that, I could
feel, and then see, all the door numbers previously invisible to me.

It was Beru who taught me to feel nature, the earth, the trees,
wind, and sky and let them carry me along as we ran from the
Shrieks. It was my first taste of what people in the Earth Realm call
magic. In Erda, they know it is the way the world works; it is the
essence of Life.

Now, as I searched for Beru, I didn't need to do anything to
see the door numbers. And even though we were indoors, I could
feel the light that the roots were radiating from where they were
hidden with the walls. So many things that I had struggled with
had become easier because Beru had been my guide.

Now, I couldn't find her. I couldn't feel her. That meant she was hiding. I stopped to think about why she would hide. I hadn't been that mean to her that morning.

Mean enough, but we had tiffs before and then laughed them off. Was it me that had hurt her, or was something else going on and I had pushed her over the edge?

We had just come from Beru's village. Had she been happy there? Thinking back, I realized that something had been wrong there too. She had looked like the beautiful flower person that she always looked like, but I wasn't sure I had heard her tinkling bell laugh. If she had laughed, it had sounded a little off. No bells. Why hadn't I noticed?

Perhaps it was because I expected her to be a little sad. Her parents hadn't returned to the village. She hadn't seen them since they left after Beru warned them about Shatterskin.

When I had first come to the Castle, Beru had berated me for not getting to know the people that were helping me. Instead, I was calling them things like Miss Floaty, Professor Pinhead, and Gazelle man. I had learned their real names after that—Aki, Professor Link, and Niko—but not much else.

We had trained, fought, laughed, worried, and planned together, but I didn't know their history. I barely knew Ruta and Beru's even though I was with them the most.

Had Ruta and Beru known me before I went to Earth? I remembered the Priscillas and Zeid, but what about everyone else?

The temptation to fall into the rabbit hole of beating myself up was so intense I had to stop and put my hand on the wall and feel the light pulsing through it. I couldn't afford that emotion. I could rectify the situation as it became appropriate, but regret was not going to defeat Deadsweep or find Beru.

Putting my hand on the wall gave me an idea. I took off my shoes and felt the earth through the Castle floor. It wasn't as hard as it might seem even though we were in a building. In Erda, everything retained its life force. Probably did in Earth too, but I didn't know to look for it when I lived there.

I walked in meditation, feeling our connection. I let my love for Beru and her strength send out waves like sonar. I stopped looking for her. Instead, I remembered that she and I were connected. It was a very different feeling than searching for a lost person.

It didn't take long before I knew where I was going. I had never been there before. I was going to Beru's room. Why hadn't I been there before? She always came to me, that's why. She did most of the work. She took care of me.

Now it was my turn to go to her, do the work of taking care of her. Whatever she needed, I would be there for her.

A few minutes later, I was standing outside a room in a hallway I never knew existed. That wasn't so unusual. The Castle was huge. Besides, I was usually either in training, planning, eating, or sleeping. There hadn't been that much time to explore.

I felt it again. That desire to be mad at myself. Why hadn't I done this before? Regret and self-recrimination were howling around me trying to get in. This time, I pretended that Pris was pulling my hair yelling at me to stop it. I smiled and knocked on the door.

The door opened by itself and I stepped into a room that reminded me of Beru's village.

Even though we were inside the Castle, there were two gardens lovingly tended on each side of the door. To get into the room itself, I walked under an arbor. Everything was blooming. The air was filled with the scent of roses and fresh earth.

I thought that the tree roots must be giving off the kind of light that these plants needed to grow, because there was only one window, although it was so big it took up almost the whole wall of the interior part of Beru's room. The curtains were closed. It was so dark I had to wait for my eyes to adjust before I could see that the room held a bed, a small table, and two chairs.

Sitting in one chair, looking as bleak as I had ever seen her, was Beru. She gestured to the other chair. As I got closer, I saw the tracks of tears running down Beru's beautiful face. This was Beru who sewed little ladybug appliques inside my leggings to remind me of my Earth mother and what she did for me. This was Beru who tried to bring happiness wherever she went.

My heart broke for her. I sat and waited. I would remain forever if I needed to.

Twenty One

I did wait a long time. We just sat there, both of us staring at the table, until finally Beru said, "Thank you for coming to find me, Hannah."

That was the second time that day that I was called by my Earth name, Hannah. When I had first found out that I was Princess Kara Beth, I never wanted to be called that. Ever. But once I realized that Princess Kara Beth was the name that inspired people to fight back against Abbadon, I accepted it. I admitted who I was and stopped resisting it. I let it be true.

However, even though it had been over six months that I had been in Erda, I was still working on that acceptance. I was accepting the fact that I had magic skills, and that I had a responsibility to save the Kingdom. I was much more reluctant to accept the latter.

The title Princess sounded lovely, but as far as I am concerned, it asks more than it gives. I didn't want to even think about what being a queen would mean. Just thinking about the responsibility and the rules freaked me out.

Sure, it might be fun to wear a crown once in a while, but I could do that for a costume party—no need to be a real queen to wear a crown.

But for Beru to call me Hannah meant something. Beru hadn't known me in Earth. Or at least I didn't think so. What did the Earth Hannah know that perhaps the Erda Kara Beth had forgotten?

The answer was so obvious that I smacked myself in the head, which made Beru giggle just a bit. She could read my mind. She knew I had remembered something I was better at doing in the Earth Realm than I was in Erda. I was a better friend. A better comforter. Yes, I had been a child in Earth, but I had understood the need for being childlike and loving without hesitation.

Since arriving in Erda, I had held back, thinking that childlike would not be princess-like. And that comforting might not be something that people wanted. I have never claimed not to be an idiot, but this realization was so fundamental I felt like one. But I laughed about it instead of being mad at myself. And then Beru laughed.

I stuck out my hand, and she slid her tiny hand on top of mine, and we wiggled our fingers at each other and laughed again. Beru laughed with tears running down her face, which on her was quite charming.

I stood up and looked around at Beru's room. There was a small kitchen against one of the walls, just like mine. "We need a cuppa," I said, pretending that it was something I always said, instead of something I heard people say and thought was cute.

I found the water, the tea, and managed to make us a cup of some floral blend that was delicious. On the way back to the table, I opened the curtains and let the sunlight stream in. From Beru's room, I could see Dalry, the village where I first met the Ginete. Perhaps a walk into the town later would be good for both of us. We could stop in to the tavern with the squeaky sign and see if people still stared at me as if I was an unwanted alien.

"Okay, Beru, talk to me," I said. "I know this can't be about me being such a jerk, although I am sure that didn't help."

When she didn't answer, I asked questions instead. I asked her about her family. What were her mother and father like? Did she get along with her parents? Was she like her parents or different? Did she have other relatives?

I had so many questions. The same kind of questions I would have asked in Earth to get to know my friends. Something I had entirely skipped over in Erda.

Yes, she missed her parents even though they never quite understood her. And no, she wasn't much like them. They were more content with how things were. She loved change. Not necessarily Abbadon type change, but change was good in Beru's eyes.

She was worried. Why hadn't she heard from her parents? No, she didn't have other relatives. She thought of Ruta as her brother. Now that was news to me. I knew the two of them were close, but not that close.

It was dinner time by the time we had finished talking. Our tea had long gone cold, but neither one of us had noticed. We had shut the door on the problems out there in the world and concentrated on being friends.

Leif was right. There had been a rift between us, but it wasn't so much the riff of what had happened, but what hadn't happened. I realized that if we were going to destroy something that infected people without their knowledge, then we were going to have to be closer than ever before.

As we walked to dinner together, Beru and I talked about the possibility that Abbadon was going to force a better world, because instead of being complacent, we were all waking up.

The people of Zerenity were realizing that they needed to practice their magic skills instead of being complacent about them.

We would all find deeper friendships within our communities. We would take better care of each other. Yes, perhaps it was being forced on us because of something that could infect us if we didn't pay attention, but we could use it for good.

"I agree with all of that, Kara Beth," Beru said. "But there is also the chance it tears us apart. If we don't know how Deadsweep infects people they might go off on their own and hide, or suspect friends and neighbors of trying to infect them. It could turn into a disaster."

"We could destroy ourselves, even without Abbadon's help," I agreed.

"So how do we stop that from happening?" Beru asked.

It was one more question that neither of us had an answer to. It could go either way. We needed much more information, and we needed it quickly.

Twenty Two

Everyone was at dinner except for Earl and Ariel. I assumed they were off commanding storms and wind where they were needed. They were both instrumental in destroying the Shrieks and Shatterskin. Earl, as Coro, had dumped a deluge of salt water on the Shrieks and Ariel, as the wind, kept pushing it the right direction until every green blob had been dissolved.

Then the Priscillas insect friends had come along and cleaned up all the green globs left lying on the ground, and that was the end of them.

I wondered briefly where all those insects had gone and shivered, thinking they might be around. When I heard the Priscillas giggle, it made me wonder. What had they done with them?

La, who didn't like misinformation being scattered around even in my imagination, pushed into my head a picture of where they were.

The Priscillas had returned them to a land far away from us. It was where they had lived before, and they were happy to return to their home. They were needed there as part of the ecosystem. Here, they would have always been looking for food sources that didn't exist.

The Priscillas had been sitting on the table waiting for me. I realized how kind it had been of them to let me go to see Beru by myself. I loved the Priscillas. Not just because they were the fairies of my dreams—what little girl didn't think about fairies—but they were smart and loyal and kept me in line. Pris was justifiably famous for her faces that could make people do things or stop doing things. I had learned early not to piss off a fairy, especially Pris.

Leif caught my eye as Beru and I came into the room together. We probably gave away the fact that our rift had been healed because we were holding hands. It was something I had never done before, and I could feel Ruta jerk back in shock. I could almost hear him say, "What, Miss High and Mighty lowers herself to holding hands?"

Ruta didn't actually dislike me. He had just formed an opinion of me when we first met that I thought too much of myself. He had been correct, of course. In turn, I had thought Ruta was the biggest grump I had ever known. I was right about that, too. But the two of us were changing, and I admired and respected Ruta, especially knowing now how much he meant to Beru.

Ruta was the healer in the group. Something I wouldn't have guessed and didn't know until after the battle with Shatterskin, when he had healed many of us. His healing abilities were something I would need to learn more about. How was Ruta healing? Why had he kept it a secret? Aki had told me it was because they didn't want him to be targeted by Abbadon. That didn't seem like the whole reason.

Beru and I didn't sit together. We had both decided to get to know the other people on our team better. I thought she was referring to me, but she assured me that there were many people in the group she didn't know well. At least not well enough to see if anything had changed, or if they needed help, or if an infection had begun.

She went to sit next to Suzanne, and I ended up next to Thomas, chosen because that's where the Priscillas had decided they wanted me to sit. It was a good idea. Although Thomas, as one of the four men from Kinver, had been around for the Shatterskin destruction, we had never really talked.

I asked him many of the same questions I had asked Beru. I asked him why he had chosen to come with us again. He said it was because of James. He had always admired James and his two brothers. John, of course, was with us, but their other brother had stayed behind to take care of the families and the family business. It was a good decision. I always thought it was idiotic that men went off to war, leaving families behind unprotected.

Thomas said he didn't have a family. Someday, he hoped to marry and have children, but for now, the adventure of going after Abbadon was what called him. "Yes," he said, "I know it's dangerous. But at the same time, I will always have these memories." Thomas waved his hand around the table, and I knew what he meant.

It was odd how sometimes evil brought people together more than good times. It was a disquieting thought, and one I tucked away for future reference.

After the metal toadstools brought us dessert, and I patted one on the head and I swear it purred at me, Sam asked me if I wanted to go into the village the next day.

Since I had just thought about how much I would like to revisit Dalry, I shouldn't have been surprised. Someone either stuck that idea into my head or picked up on it. But Sam, a Ginete, asking me? Pita was the Ginete we dealt with the most because he was, as he called himself, the head brother. So Sam asking me instead of Pita meant something. Plus, although the first time I had met the Ginete was in the village, I had the impression that the town was a little leery of them.

"Oh, they still are," Sam said. "It's kind of fun to mess with them."

Seeing my confusion, Zeid stepped in. "We're all going, Kara. Or at least most of us. And yes, we're messing with your expectations. Or at least Pita and his brothers are."

I looked over at the Ginete brothers. They always reminded me of a combination lighthouse with their huge eyes and a dwarf, or maybe ET. But I was warned never to call them dwarfs. I didn't want to see what would happen if I did. What I did know is that they were crucial to the success of our last mission. Not fighters. Providers. They enabled us to do what we needed to do.

"Aren't we supposed to be stopping Deadsweep?" I asked, thinking how much I would like to go to the village, but worried it was taking us away from our work.

"Yes. We are," Niko answered. "And going into the village might yield us some answers."

"I'm in!" I said, raising my water glass. I looked across at Zeid, ready to ask another question. He made a slight gesture with his head, which told me to be quiet for now. Yes, that gesture told me there is more to this than meets the eye, but wait and see what it is.

My curiosity was going full blast, but I was exhausted. I could wait until the next day to find out what no one was saying out loud. I thought that it was probably a good thing I didn't know yet. It turned out that for once I was right.

TWENTY THREE

If I thought I would escape my training sessions the next day with Niko, Aki, and Professor Link, I was mistaken. But this time, it wasn't brutal. They had made their point about being too tired to think and how vulnerable it had made me. How being too tired made everyone vulnerable.

Instead, the training felt good. Zeid and I had a chance to practice our sparring skills together. I didn't fall on my face as much as I used to, and I even earned a high five from Niko, something I had never gotten before.

Aki gave me new exercises to increase my flexibility, which at times made me feel as if I was going to break in half. I didn't need a high five from Aki in her class to feel good. I loved it enough to go without being told to. Besides, she knew how to do something I dreamed about doing—levitating.

Although I now knew how to fly very short distances, I couldn't levitate the way she could.

On the other hand, I didn't know anyone else who could either. Maybe it was specific to Aki's people. I planned to find a way to ask her all the questions that friends ask each other, but I wasn't at all that sure that she would answer them. But I had to try.

Link spent time in class reviewing how to close our mental doors and communication channels. He kept sending mental suggestions to Zeid and me, and we were supposed to keep them away. It was so hard. It's actually easier to block a physical weapon than a mental one. One is easier to see I guess. I thought it was great information, but I wanted to know if he really believed that Deadsweep would get into our heads that way.

"It's a good point, Kara," Link said. "We don't know how it is happening. But it never hurts to get better at recognizing false suggestions."

By the end of the session, I managed to stop him a few times, but that was because I began to recognize his pattern. Although he used different "voices," he still spoke in a certain way and used the same kind of phrases. Once I recognized that pattern, I could detect his influence.

After class, Link sat on the edge of his desk and addressed Zeid and me. I used to call him Professor Pinhead because he was so long and lanky. Link often wore his black hair slicked back like a helmet. When he wanted to make a point, Link would squint his green eyes at you.

Sitting on the edge of his desk, he started squinting before speaking. "Both of you did well with this, but that's because you now know me. That's a good thing. And that's a bad thing. Someone could use my pattern of speaking to you to make you think it's me.

"Plus, we don't know the voice, or pattern, that Deadsweep's suggestions take."

I tried not to be disrespectful when I asked, "How come you don't? Shouldn't you have some idea by now?" But even I could hear the hint of sarcasm in the question.

I almost said, "Sorry," but Link held up his hand to stop me. "Yes, we should," he said, and walked out of the room.

"Don't," I said to Zeid, as he turned to speak. "I shouldn't have said that. I'm sure everyone has been working hard on this question."

"And with no answers," Zeid replied. "But that's why we are going into the village. There have been some disturbances. We're going to investigate them, and perhaps get a clue as to what is going on."

I wanted to start for the village of Dalry that very minute, but it was another few hours before we gathered outside the Castle and began the walk to town.

Last time we walked this way, I had been clueless as to how people in Erda did things. I had forgotten so many things while living in the Earth Realm. This time was different. I knew more. However, I felt as if I knew too many things that didn't fit together. We were in the phase of too little knowledge, which I knew was dangerous.

Leif and Sarah weren't walking with us. I hadn't expected them to come into town. They were continually disappearing and reappearing. I suppose they had other things they needed to do.

Teddy also wasn't with us. He scared some people, so it was better he stayed away. It was funny because of all of us, Teddy was probably the most gentle. Like the Ginete, he didn't fight; he provided. He and his friends built the tunnels that we lived in when we needed to escape the Shrieks.

Although they didn't look like each other, the Ginete and the Whistle Pigs were cousins. They both lived underground, and it was the Whistle Pigs who built their underground homes and tunnels. The Ginete stayed in the Whistle Pigs' tunnels and rooms while keeping us safe, but I knew that the Ginete preferred their home in the sides of hills and mountains.

I had never seen those homes, but Sam had said they looked similar to the rooms where we had stayed. Above the ground, the tree roots were hidden in the walls. Underground, they were visible as they held the dirt walls together and provided the light and energy needed.

The Ginete and the Whistle Pigs were also the technicians that had built the shields we needed to stun the Shrieks. After the last battle, we had left the shields with the Whistle Pigs. If we needed them again, they were available, but I didn't see how they could help with Deadsweep's mental virus.

Only Pita came with us to the village. I still didn't know the story why sometimes the villagers both respected the Ginete and were a little standoffish, too. But I figured that's why only one Ginete came with us.

We were a motley crew strolling down the road. High above us, Lady circled along with two other pileated dragons. I couldn't tell all of them apart except for Lady, probably because Lady was also Suzanne. I knew that once we got to town, the two dragons would keep watch while Suzanne came into town with us.

Ruta and Beru walked behind us. Zeid was on my right, and Cahir, having made it to the Castle the day before, now walked on my left. I loved dropping my hand into his fur and leaving it there while we walked.

Cahir never indicated whether he liked my hand on him or not, but I assumed if he didn't, he wouldn't hesitate to let me know. Besides, he seemed to enjoy the Priscillas riding on him. La likes to sit on Cahir's head and hold on to his ear. Pris likes to fly ahead and come back to check on us. She has a hard time keeping still. Cil loves burying herself inside Cahir's fur so that sometimes she isn't visible at all. Except every once in a while the tip of her wing peeks out and catches the sun, turning it into a petal of rainbows.

Link, Aki, and Niko took turns walking in front and then in the back. It looked like a casual walk, but watching how alert everyone was behaving gave it away. The four men from Kinver guarded the two sides and the back.

Yes, it was a pleasant walk, but not for a minute did anyone think that we were safe. We didn't know what form Deadsweep took to infect. We didn't know if it was one thing or many. We didn't know if one of us was already infected. No wonder although we laughed and chatted, we weren't relaxed.

I hoped that the village would bring the answer to at least one question.

Twenty Four

We did get one question answered. We found out what the aftermath of infection looked like. After seeing it, and discovering that it was the result of only three people, the terror of the Deadsweep began to sink in.

The once quiet town of Dalry, with its well-tended lawns and gardens, was gone. Oh, it was still quiet. Very quiet. Nobody was out. Instead of neighbors chatting together or strolling the streets there was no one in sight. The way the town looked, it appeared no one had ventured out for a long time. All the windows and doors were closed, and I was sure that for the first time, they were locked.

What had caused the fear was not readily apparent. Link turned on the communication channel between all of us, in case we would need it. Everyone gave him a thumbs up when he asked if we were all on. Lady landed beside Cahir and then turned into Suzanne. Forgetting the channel, I spoke out loud, "What the zonk?"

"Well said," Suzanne answered, which caused a titter of laughter.

The tavern's sign was still squeaking as we headed there. As we got closer, we could hear voices, loud voices and breaking glass. In the Earth Realm, this might have been a normal sound coming from a tavern as people drank too much and started fighting. In Erda, no one drank too much, and before Abbadon began his campaign of destruction, no one fought either.

The martial arts forms that Niko had been teaching us were used for physical conditioning in Erda, not for fighting. Niko had fallen in love with them as a youngster and studied with a master who had moved away years before. Now we learned those forms to defend ourselves. As we heard more glass breaking, I was happy I had at least learned the basics.

Niko had told us to split up on each side of the tavern door. One group would go in first, and the other group would cover them. It was possible that what was going on was all being done as a bit of fun. Not likely, but possible, and we didn't want to stir up trouble if it was innocent.

Just as Niko gave the signal to go in, the tavern door banged open, and a man flew out, landing on his back in the street. Two other men followed him with what looked like small tree trunks in their hands. It was obvious they were heading to the man on the street who already looked as if he had been beaten with something.

Before we could stop what was happening, the Priscillas attacked the two men's faces. Pris took the lead man and punched him in both eyes. Cil and La each took an eye of the other one.

I was stunned. I didn't know that the Priscillas were fighters. Although I should have realized, given how many times they had pulled my hair or berated me for my idiocy. Still, it was awesome to watch the two men drop, screaming.

Suzanne had turned back into a dragon and landed on the men in the street. Her talons held two of them down, and she pinned the third under her wing.

When I went to help, Zeid yelled, "Don't touch them!"

Beru pulled a fine net out of her pocket, which I had never seen before, and we all helped spread it over the men as Lady backed off of them.

Niko had taken the first group into the tavern and reported that there was no one else in there, so we pulled the net tight and led the three men back in.

We stared in shock. Inside, the tavern was destroyed. Everything was broken or shattered into tiny bits.

"Do you like it, smartass?" one man yelled, snarling at Niko. "We did it. You think you have stopped us, but you haven't. There are a lot of us. You can stop us three, but you can't stop the army that is forming."

These men talking that way was so out of context of everything I knew about Erda that I couldn't speak. But then no one else did either. What was there to say?

Aki had left and returned with a man who we had met the last time we had been here. Although now he looked entirely different. His face was pale, and his clothes hung on him.

"Ah, Mayor!" the younger man shouted. "You little coward. What's your town going to do now, huh? What if there are more of us out there, just waiting to explode. What if you are one of them, and you don't know yet?"

Mayor Tom blanched and ran out of the room, which only caused the men to taunt him more. It didn't matter that they were firmly bound up in a net. They had one thing on their minds. Make us all afraid. They were doing an outstanding job of it.

Niko looked up as Pita entered the room with his brother Sam. They were carrying a container filled with hoses, and what looked like a tarp. Niko nodded at the Ginete and shooed the rest of the team out of the tavern.

"Do you know what's happening in there?" we all asked Professor Link.

"The Ginete have prepared a gas that will put those men to sleep. Once it is all set up, they will come out here and wait until the gas disperses."

Looking at our shocked faces, he added, "No, it won't hurt them. We just need to get them to a safe place without any of us touching them, and the Ginete suggested this."

"What if it doesn't work?" I asked. Leave it to me to ask the question everyone was thinking.

"We'll make it stronger."

Pita, Sam, and Niko came out looking as terrible as the rest of us. These were people, not green globs and a metal robot.

We all moved to the other side of the street just in case some of the gas leaked. Mayor Tom invited us to his house to wait, which most of us were happy to do, including me.

Once the gas was gone, the Ginete, Niko, and Zeid slid a wagon under the soundly sleeping bundled men. They pulled the cart into a side street. Right before it disappeared underground, I saw the ring around the circle that the Whistle Pigs had developed. Those magic circles had saved us more than once. Now they were going to save us in a different way.

"Now what?" I asked.

"Now we interview everyone, but first, since we don't know how the infection spreads, we need to take precautions," Aki said.

"For me, too?" squeaked the Mayor.

"Yes, for you, too," Aki assured him.

Who could blame him? His town was under attack by an unknown and unseen enemy. I was trying to keep a brave face, but from the moment I saw the men, I was terrified. Evil had come to Dalry.

TWENTY FIVE

We set ourselves up in the Mayor's home. His wife asked if we were hungry, and although I knew everyone was, we all turned her down. We suspected that their food supplies were short due to the invasion of Deadsweep into their town, and we didn't want to deplete them further. Later I thought that perhaps it was also because we thought the food might contain the infection. Anything was possible.

We were all wearing something that looked like a spacesuit, but it wasn't clumsy like the ones I remembered our astronauts using. They were comfortable and fit like our regular clothes. The Priscillas were the ones responsible for the material, but they wouldn't say what it was or where they got it. I had a suspicion it was from the fairy community, and that meant we might never know. Fairies keep their secrets.

The Whistle Pigs had fitted us up with one of their technology gadgets that we were to breathe through. Once again, they were coming to our rescue with their technical wizardry.

"Shouldn't we have had these on when we first came in?" I asked, smarty pants me thinking of something after the fact.

I got the evil look I deserved from Pris. Well, actually from everyone. So I shut up and listened.

It was hard to coax the villagers out of their homes, but the Mayor assured them that the men were gone and that we were there to stop any further infection.

He was lying of course. We were there to stop any further infection, but we had no idea how to do it, or if it was already present in people. The hope was by asking about the three men we would get a clue as to where they had picked up the Deadsweep virus, as we were calling it. Of course, we were guessing again. Was it a virus? Or was it an injection of something?

We questioned everyone. Although we tried to make it as pleasant as possible, the fact that we were wearing protective clothing and they weren't didn't help our public image. But most of the villagers understood we were trying to stop what was happening and gave us as much information as they knew, which wasn't much.

All three men were loved and respected in the community. One of the men had a wife, Letha, and two daughters. They were devastated. It felt as if one minute they had a loving father and husband and the next he was angry and throwing things.

It was that man's family that was the most helpful because they had an eye on him every day. One of his little girls mentioned that a few days before he had started getting mean, which wasn't like him at all. It scared her. He would snap at her for simple things that he usually loved to do, like read her a book before bed. Once she heard her daughter mention her husband's irritability, Letha said she noticed those things too. Tiny things, but not the way he usually acted. And, yes, it had been a few days before it got worse. Before he stormed out of the house and started terrorizing the town.

After hearing that, we went back to the friends of the other two men and heard basically the same story. It wasn't an overnight explosion into anger. It was a progression. They didn't have a context in which to put the irritability, so they ignored it. People in Erda were not easily irritated. At least they weren't before.

By the time we had questioned everyone, we were exhausted. And we knew we had to interview everyone again. However, we had to figure out how to interview for the appearance of irritability without suggesting it.

The other thing we were looking for was rifts within relationships. But once again we were worried about causing something by suggesting that it might be present. If we suggested they were irritable, wouldn't that start a rift? And if that was what let the infection in, wouldn't we be the ones that caused it?

It was so tricky we decided not to do any more of that kind of questioning that day. Lady had flown back to the Castle and arranged a delivery of food for Dalry so we left the village, saying we would be back with more information as soon as possible.

Before we left, we asked a few more straightforward questions. Were the three men friends? Did they hang out together? Had they gone anywhere together different from anyone else in the village had?

We couldn't give them a timeline. We didn't know if the infection set in and waited, or immediately started acting. The answers we got from the villagers were, "Yes, they were friends, but then who wasn't?" The villagers weren't kidding. They were all friends. To the question, "Did they go somewhere together?" no one knew the answer. So we asked them to ask around and report back to the Mayor, and he would follow up on the information.

"You mean to be like a detective they have in Earth?" he asked me.

"How do you know about detectives?" I asked.

"Suzanne would tell us stories sometimes about things that went on there. Being a detective seemed pointless before. What was there to detect? Now I see how it could be valuable."

I high-fived him. He had perked up in the past few hours and seemed genuinely interested in finding the information that we needed.

However, before we left, I overheard Niko speaking with Mayor Tom, warning him that he needed to be on the lookout for unusual behavior in others, including with himself. Niko handed the Mayor a device that would connect him immediately with our team.

"You have to tell us right away, Tom," Niko said. "We might not be able to stop it, but for sure we could keep you from harming others until we can get rid of the infection."

Mayor Tom returned to being pale. He slumped and mumbled that he understood. Who could blame him? No matter how you looked at it, this infection was horrendous. I could see how the name Deadsweep was appropriate. It caused the death of the person everyone knew. I hoped it didn't cause actual death.

But it did. By the time we arrived underground, where the Whistle Pigs were keeping the men, one of them was dead.

TWENTY SIX

No sooner had we all descended via the circles into the Whistle Pigs underground rooms did we hear crying. Loud crying. No one met us in the transportation room, so after taking off our suits and air filters, we made our way down the hall to where the sound was coming from.

We found Teddy with Pita and his brother standing in the hallway. The Ginete were the ones who were crying. Huge tears were running down their faces. Their bright golden eyes were dark and swollen.

Teddy was doing his best to comfort them, but it didn't seem to be working.

"What's going on?" Niko asked, pulling Teddy away from the Ginete while the rest of us stood by looking helpless.

Teddy lowered his voice and said, "One of the men died."

"What! How?" Niko whispered back, but it sounded like yelling, anyway.

"We took the net off of them once we got down here and put them into a room by themselves. They were still asleep from the gas, so we thought we had time to put them into separate rooms, which we were still getting ready for them.

"We were only gone a minute or two, but when we got back, the two men that had been beating on the first man woke up and attacked him again."

"With what? Surely you didn't leave them with weapons."

"Of course not," Teddy humphed. "It's worse than that. They use their hands, their heads, their teeth ...."

"Their teeth?" I said, horrified.

Teddy nodded. "It's more horrible than you can imagine."

I didn't think that could be true since I was imagining a gruesome death, but I decided to not see for myself.

"We have put the remaining two men into separate rooms. They seem calm for now. Maybe the killing let off some of the poison in their system."

"Or maybe Deadsweep just needs time to recharge," Aki said. She had been standing by quietly listening to what was going on, although, like me, she had grown pale.

The Ginete had calmed a bit and were no longer sobbing, but they still looked miserable. I had never seen the Ginete helpless like that.

"Why were the Ginete so upset?" I asked.

"They think it's their fault that the gas didn't keep the men asleep longer," Teddy answered.

Leif and Sarah appeared and put their arms around the Ginete and walked them away. I knew they couldn't be in better hands. They would help them understand it wasn't their fault. It wasn't anyone's fault. No one knew how this infection was going to work.

There was only one person at fault. Abbadon. The creator of monsters, a monster himself.

We were all directed by the Whistle Pigs to head to our rooms and to take a shower using some special soap that they had put there for us. Who knew if that would do anything? We were entirely in the dark about what Deadsweep was and how it spread. But I enjoyed the feeling of the hot water rushing across my body. I tried to imagine it washing away the memories of what we saw in the village and the horror of what Teddy had described.

It helped, but I knew the memory would never go away. It would be part of the Abbadon horror story as long as I lived.

We met in the planning room. Although it wasn't the same planning room we had met in to discuss how to stop the Shrieks and Shatterskin, it looked exactly the same.

The Whistle Pigs designed all their places to look the same. In one way it was very comforting. We knew what to expect. On the other hand, it was disconcerting. Who knew where we were? There was no sun or moon or stars or landmarks to tell me if we were directly under the village of Dalry or somewhere far away.

Aki took pity on me and told me that we were between Dalry and the Castle, and would be staying underground until we knew more, or as we had to deal with things topside.

The Castle staff had been alerted and told that the Castle was going to be sealed off from the outside starting that day. They had let the staff know that they could bring their families into the Castle with them if they wanted. It turned out many of them already lived there, something I didn't know, once again proving to me that I was not paying attention to the people around me.

In the planning room, the Ginete brothers were leaning against the wall looking a little better, but their sparkle had not returned. They had refused to sit. They often refused to sit down. It was part of their nature to be alert, and that was working against them this time because they were taking on a responsibility that wasn't theirs.

I understood how they felt though. I think we all did. But I was worried. Wasn't this a form of a rift? Weren't we all responsible for how the Ginete felt?

Niko turned to me and said, "Yes, it is a rift, Kara. And yes, we are all responsible for how we all feel."

Turning to Pita, he said, "You couldn't have known. We have never dealt with this before. Let's look at what you did do. You eliminated the danger to the village. You kept us all safe from them. Who knows? If it hadn't happened this time, they would have found another way. Let it go."

The Ginete nodded, and I could tell they were trying to pull themselves out of the grief, when I noticed Leif pull his staff to him, and touch it gently on the ground. I could see the blue haze I had felt before running along the floor of our room and up into the wall behind the Ginete, encircling each one of them like a halo around their entire body.

The haze dissipated in a flash, and I was fairly sure none of the Ginete had seen it happen, but all five brothers were immediately back to themselves. Maybe everyone else in the room had noticed and were not acknowledging it, or perhaps Leif was only showing me. Either way, it made me wish that I had that kind of ability.

Throwing lightning bolts was awesome, but to heal like that? I wanted to be part of it. Ruta leaned over and whispered in my ear, "It's possible, Kara Beth." Ruta, who only spoke when necessary, had just given me a gift I could cherish. Ruta was a healer, too.

I smiled at him, and I swear he smiled back. I thought back to when I had thought of Ruta as a wooden stump and secretly called him Block Face. I wondered if the world had felt the shift between us. Abbadon could do its worst, but I knew we could stop him. We had each other.

TWENTY SEVEN

In spite of the Ginete's improved attitude, the meeting was somber. Especially after we realized that the murdered man was Letha's husband. I couldn't imagine how terrible Letha and her daughters were going to feel, and I wondered who was going to tell them.

"You are, Princess," Niko said.

I wanted to protest, or at least pout, but I knew that Niko was right. It was me, their princess, who had to tell the two little girls that their father had died at the hands of his friends, and no one knew why.

It was impossible to ask the two men. After being docile for about an hour after killing their friend, they started screaming again and ended up slamming themselves up against the walls of their room.

The Ginete had experimented with piping in different levels of gas and had finally found one that would keep the men quiet, but not put them to sleep. However, if we were going to save them, Ruta would have to examine them somehow.

For now, it was decided only to observe, and perhaps get them to talk through the intercom that the Whistle Pigs had set up in their rooms. The danger of infection was too high to do anything else.

They had left the dead man in his room, and the temperature dropped to below freezing. Although it would have been good to examine him, and then return him to his family, we had no idea what we might be releasing. Things like autopsies were an Earth thing, not an Erda experience.

By the time we had worked out all these provisions, the night was half over. It had been the worst day ever. It started pleasantly enough and ended up with one dead man, and two others in desperate condition. We all needed rest if we were going to be of any use the next day.

As I headed off to my room with Beru by my side, I realized that I couldn't go to my room yet.

"I need to know more," I whispered to Beru.

She gave me one of her famous looks, but this one had a hint of compassion in it. "Still the curious one, aren't you? You know curiosity can get you in trouble?" Beru whispered back.

"I've heard that. I think people say that nonsense to keep us from knowing things we should know. Sometimes it can cause trouble, but most of the time, curiosity can discover what needs to be known. I think it's a good trade-off," I answered, as if I was a wise one.

Beru laughed a weak version of her tinkling bell laugh. "Okay, I'll give you that one, young lady, but do us all a favor and think first?"

"I'm thinking," I said as I walked faster down the hall. "I'm thinking I want to see."

Beru quick stepped to catch up with me. She didn't need to ask me where I was going. I was reasonably sure that she was planning to do the same thing once she dropped me off at my room. I wondered if she also planned to lock me in like she used to just for fun since she knew I had learned how to unlock doors at the wave of my hand.

We reached the doors where we were going. These were doors I had no desire to unlock. I just wanted to see inside.

The first room was where the dead man was laying. The Whistle Pigs had installed a window in the three doors. Not the usual thing for them. And they had to be careful not to make it reflective. Everyone knew that Abbadon used mirrors to see what was going on in the rest of Erda. But no one was sure if it was all reflective surfaces or just mirrors.

I missed mirrors, although there was a good side to not having any. I didn't worry about what I looked like even though I hadn't seen myself since I fell through the portal and discovered I was a young woman in Erda instead of the twelve-year-old girl I had been in the Earth dimension.

On the other hand, not having seen myself, I was never sure if I looked okay. But everyone had the same problem. If someone's clothes needed adjusting, or their hair was not quite right, people stepped in. No embarrassment. It was just a helping hand.

The dead man inside the room was never going to have a helping hand again. He lay there where he had been beaten. Teddy had told me not to look and I understood why. More than half his face gone. Bitten off, I guess. There was no way I was going to tell his family that. They should remember him as he was before—before Deadsweep.

I could feel the coldness of the room even though it was a well-sealed door. I pressed my hand up against the glass and promised the man inside that we would find out what happened. It wasn't an idle promise. We had to find out.

Beru and I moved to another room that was the holding cell for one of the prisoners. Prisoners, an utterly unfamiliar term in the Kingdom of Zerenity. There had never been a need for someone to be locked up. Sometimes people got into light-hearted trouble, expressing themselves in ways that may not have been the wisest, but the community always took care of it.

I hated the idea that we had to lock these men up. We might need prisons for now. But I hoped the prisons would go away after we stopped Abbadon.

If I thought I would be angry at the men who killed their friend, one look at them and I knew it wasn't their fault. They were out of their minds. The gas was keeping them docile, but the agitation that ran through them was like a live current.

"We haven't been able to get them to eat," Aki said, slipping up beside us. We hadn't heard her coming. That was Aki. Not for the first time I was glad she was on "our side." Quiet and calm, Aki was also cunning, and I suspected she was capable of things other than levitating and showing up wherever she wanted to. Not that those two things weren't enough.

The three of us stood at the door, watching the man inside go not so quietly crazy.

"We'll fix this," Beru whispered. Aki and I nodded in agreement.

TWENTY EIGHT

The next morning, I met Zeid in the transportation room. At the meeting the night before he had volunteered to go with me. I knew that everyone approved. After all, at some point he would be my husband, and that would make him a Prince. Or something like that. It occurred to me I had no idea what he would become when we married. But then I didn't even know when we were getting married, or if it was an arranged marriage or if we had chosen each other. It was still something that existed back in my memories, and no one seemed inclined to fill me in, including Zeid.

What I knew was that I was happy that it was Zeid who would be my husband. The more I spent time around Zeid, even if it wasn't just the two of us, the more I liked him. I could have said, loved him, but I wanted to like him first, and I did. Love, maybe, but we didn't have time for that right now. He knew it. I knew it.

At the moment, what was important was that I wasn't going alone. Maybe it was Zeid's responsibility, but I couldn't have been happier that he wanted to come with me. It certainly wasn't romantic. But at least we were doing something together. Something important. Something I wasn't so sure I could do by myself. I wasn't even sure I could do it with him. All I knew was it had to be done.

The suits we had left in the transport room were waiting for us, but something had changed. I stopped in the doorway and stared.

I heard the Priscillas giggling as they all flew in the room yelling, "Surprise!" Perhaps it wasn't a big deal, but what they had done meant so much to me, I started to cry.

"How did you do that?" I asked through my happy tears.

"Magic. You know magic, don't you, Kara Beth?" Cil teased. La and Pris giggled again with her and flew to my suit which the day before had been a stark white. Today it was a lovely mauve shade. Actually, all the suits were now different colors. Zeid had an azure blue one, matching his eyes. I looked at Cil, and she giggled. They knew what they were doing. The song "Matchmaker, Matchmaker," popped into my head. Cil winked at me.

"We started with you, Kara Beth," La said. "We knew how hard this was going to be for you, so we wanted to make it cheerier. Then we realized the town would feel better if you all showed up in colors instead of white, looking so stern and scary.

"But we did something special to your suit," Pris said. She flew down to my hand and pulled me over to where my suit was hanging and then turned up the cuff and showed me the ladybug appliqué. That did it. I really started crying. I was so happy I didn't even think about being embarrassed.

Zeid stood there looking confused, but pleased. "You are happy, right?" he asked.

When I nodded yes, he looked relieved and stepped back as I hugged the Priscillas the best that I could. They are little wiggly creatures, all wings and fluttery. But I managed to kiss all three on the cheek before they got away. I had to let them know how much their thoughtfulness meant to me.

Plus, they were right. It was going to be better showing up in colors. Nothing we had to say to the people of Dalry would make anyone happy, but at least our suits wouldn't be so scary.

After getting our suits on, we added the improved breathers and goggles that had appeared there overnight—another gift from the ingenious Whistle Pigs and Ginete working together. I couldn't figure out which of them made what. They seemed to need each other to make something happen.

The symbolism of that didn't escape me. We all needed each other to accomplish anything. What did Abbadon need to make Deadsweep work? He wanted to be alone, but he wasn't really. He used the energy of his captives to run his machines and keep his environment going as he destroyed everything else. He wanted to think of himself as alone. But he wasn't. So what did he need to work with to have something like the Deadsweep? It was a question I thought we needed to answer. Perhaps later when we returned.

At that moment the question was what could I say to Letha and her daughters that would mean anything. That would comfort them, and give them hope. Nothing would replace the man they loved. And we knew nothing about how or why he died.

At the meeting, we had decided not to tell them how horrible his death had been. What would it serve? If we were able to rid the two men of the infection, how would they ever be accepted into their village again if the town knew what they had done? Would it matter that it was something else that had made them act that way? There was a chance we would have to keep them separate from everyone for the rest of their lives.

The problem was, it was not just these three men. Deadsweep could be anywhere in the Kingdom. Friends and neighbors, husbands, wives, and maybe children could become infected. They would become someone else. Would we ever be able to return things to the harmony of how things were before?

No one knew. I reached out for Zeid's hand and nodded to the Whistle Pig who was standing by to lift us to the surface. All I knew at that moment was I was going to have to grow up a little bit more. Niko was right. It was up to me. Not only did I have to help save the Kingdom, but I also had to help find a way to heal it.

TWENTY NINE

We arrived topside a little way outside the village. I could see the Castle shining in the distance. It looked like a castle I had seen in one of my story books in the Earth Realm. A valley. A castle. All we needed was a rainbow and a dancing queen, and I would be in that story. Except there was no evil in that childhood fairy tale. No Abbadon the destroyer.

Not for the first time, I wondered why Abbadon was so intent on taking away all this beauty. Yes, Aki had told me the story of the two bored brothers on the serpent-shaped spaceship who decided to experiment with the two dimensions of Erda and Earth. Just for fun. Right.

Maybe if they had stayed on the planet Gaia they would have been disabused of that idea. Why experiment with this harmony and perfectness? Perhaps the trees would have had time to heal them of their boredom and desire to control. Maybe they would have leaned down and whacked them on the head with a big heavy branch and been done with all the craziness before it started.

Come to think of it, why didn't they? Nature is alive. Why not stop the infection—which in this case was two bored brothers—before it started? Questions with no answers.

While all these whys rolled around in my head, Zeid and I stood there hand in hand enjoying the glorious sunshine, the gentle breeze, and the whispering of the leaves as they moved with the wind. It was so perfect I almost forgot why we had come.

"Daydreaming, Kara Beth?" Zeid asked.

"More like trying to understand how anyone could want to destroy all this."

"Any closer to understanding?"

I shook my head no.

"Maybe Abbadon is infected too," Zeid answered.

I looked at him and shook my head again. "No. I can't let him get away with that excuse. He deliberately destroys. He knows what he is doing. He's not out of control the way those poor men are."

"Maybe it's a different kind of infection. Something to keep in mind, since, in the end, we will have to go after him."

It was something to keep in mind. Maybe evil was an infection. So how to stop it? Why did it exist in the first place? Because two bored brothers brought it here? Were they infected?

I almost touched the star around my neck. I wanted to see the beauty of the intertwined life that existed but was invisible to most people most of the time. But Liza told me to practice seeing without it. I didn't have to tell Zeid what I wanted to do. He waited while I breathed, calmed myself down, and unfocused from seeing the world that was in front of me. I wanted to see the world that existed beyond the visible world, but was always present.

Like with the magic-picture books, as my view shifted, the whole world refocused into something even more beautiful than I had just been seeing. More color, more grace, more interconnection. The depth that existed below our normal view was always so stunning I could only stay for a few moments.

When it was over, I stood silently letting the tears run down my face.

"That beautiful?" Zeid asked.

"More than that, Zeid. It's more than the word beautiful and it's right here. Nature knows it, lives there. We only see the tip of it, live on the surface of it. Imagine what it would be like to live within that all the time.

"Do you think it's possible?" Zeid asked.

I didn't have an answer to that. We did live there. We just didn't see it or know it most of the time. It was a rabbit hole I couldn't allow myself to go down. We had something important to do. The glorious hidden-within-plain-sight world would have to wait. We had bad news to deliver.

For a moment we wondered if perhaps we had come to the wrong village. Everything was so different from what we had seen the day before.

There were people in the streets. Some were even smiling. I noticed that they stayed a little further apart from each other, still not knowing how the infection spread. But at least they were out, walking the streets, fixing their gardens, and shopping.

Seeing Zeid and I were walking in wearing our suits, goggles, and breathers wasn't going to be inviting to them, but there was nothing we could do about that. Even though the breathers were almost invisible, the suits pretty, and the goggles stylish, we were still reminders of the danger.

There was another danger. How would the villagers know it was us? We could be someone who meant to do them harm. Although I knew that it was unlikely that someone could copy the technology of the suits, they could duplicate the look.

"We have thought of that, Kara Beth," Link pushed into my head. "Let's hope we discover soon how the infection spreads, and it doesn't involve wearing suits.

"I don't want to hurry the two of you talking to the family, but if you could get it done and get back, we would all feel better about it."

I said, "Roger that!" and laughed. Link did not.

As we walked into town, I thought again how much I loved these little villages with their English cottages crossed with a Hobbit look. In good times this would be the perfect town to visit and have a cup of coffee in the garden.

Today was not so pleasant. As soon as someone saw us walking into town, the people rushed us for information. The Mayor shouldered his way through the crowd and Zeid quietly whispered that we were there to see the wife and children we had met yesterday.

The Mayor knew why we were there. When I first met him, I hadn't realized he was so perceptive. Perhaps he hadn't been then.

Once he walked us to the cottage where the man's family was, the whole crowd stopped. They knew. Some of the women went back to their homes. I knew what they were doing. They went to get food or anything else they thought the widow and her children would need.

I had never told someone that the one they loved had died. I never thought it would be something I had to do. I never wanted to do it again. The moment when all the light went out of his wife's face was horrible. I knew that she was hoping it was good news, and then seeing the tears in my eyes she knew it wasn't. It was as if something sucked the life out of her.

The children just stared. How could they understand? Nothing like this had happened before, but I knew it would happen again. That's what made it worse.

As we left, the crowd opened for us and let us through, even though no one acknowledged us. I was glad. I wanted to be invisible. Everything had changed. The world that had been bright and colorful had turned gray.

THIRTY

We met in the conference room. Link had called us all there, so I thought that he was going to run the meeting. I thought it would be the professor who would tell us what we were doing. At least I hoped he knew what we were doing.

Instead, the two people standing at the head of the table were Pita and Teddy, looking both grim and satisfied at the same time. But then you had to know them well to understand what they were thinking.

One thing I had to learn as I met new species like the Ginete and the Whistle Pigs was to determine how to tell them apart from each other, let alone know what they were thinking from their facial expressions. It sounds terrible, but it's true. Humans are not good at recognizing the differences in other species.

And humans are a strange species. We don't look alike. It's so rare to resemble someone else that everyone exclaims over it. We are fat, tall, skinny, wide, with different facial shapes, a variety of skin colors, and even more hair types. We speak multiple languages with an amazing variety of accents. But we know how to tell ourselves apart in spite of the fact we are all so different.

I hadn't thought about the fact that other species looked mostly the same to me until one day I tried to determine if I was looking at Lady or another pileated dragon. I couldn't decide if it was her or not, and she wasn't giving me the clue of shapeshifting back into Suzanne. I had to concentrate on what I was looking at. And then

I saw the little differences that made her Lady. After that, it was much easier.

It was the same with the Ginete brothers. I knew Pita was the oldest and the tallest. After spending time with Tita, I knew he had a softer feel, and his golden eyes were darker and more rounded than his brothers. Once I started noticing these differences, I got better at seeing the difference between all of the brothers.

So far, Teddy was the easiest of the Whistle Pigs because he was the one that talked to me and called me made up names. I hadn't gotten to know the rest of the Whistle Pigs very well. They were often busy in the tunnels, building and maintaining. It was because of those tireless workers that we had been saved from the Shrieks and Shatterskin. I appreciated them even if it was from afar.

The Whistle Pigs didn't live in the tunnels and rooms where we spent our time. They had their own homes further below. And when the Ginete had a choice, they preferred homes in mountains and hills. However, everything was different since Abbadon decided to rule the world.

Now their villages were often found in these tunnels, which were also common ground to both the Ginete and the Whistle Pigs, and a safe place for the rest of us.

Zeid and I were the last to arrive. Usually, there would be talking and joking while waiting for a meeting to begin. Not this time. The room was deadly silent.

"What the ziffer is going on?" I blurted out. That's me. A big mouth. Can't keep myself from saying what's on my mind.

Only Teddy responded with a tiny smile and a whisper, "Good afternoon to you, Twinkle Face."

I smiled back at him, grateful for the encouragement in what was promising to be a disturbing meeting.

Link gestured at Pita to begin. It was apparent that he wanted to and didn't want to at the same time.

Finally, letting out a huge sigh, he said, "Well, here's the good news. We don't think you need to wear the suits anymore."

"So it's not an infection transferred through touch or air or fluids or...?"

I was stopped from continuing by Pita, holding up his hand.

"Fair enough, Kara Beth. You come from a dimension where the belief is that infections spread that way, so you are aware of the many ways it can happen."

"Wait. Belief? That's how it happens." I snapped.

Link stepped in. "I don't think this is a productive topic of conversation. But as unifying thought, let's say this: it's like those open doors we are always talking about, Kara. Until those doors are shut, and rifts healed, things get in."

I nodded. I understood that I was leading everyone off topic, but I wanted to pursue what Pita said another time. I did understand the open doors. And rifts inside ourselves. At least I was aware of the need to understand them, anyway. It was a start.

"Sorry, Pita," I apologized. "You were saying?"

Pita took another deep breath. I wasn't sure whether he was recovering from my interruption or upset by what he was going to tell us. Once we heard what he had to say, I knew it was more than the latter.

"No, we don't think Deadsweep enters the system in any of those ways that you mentioned, Kara. Although, we are not one hundred percent sure. Because what we saw could not have entered the bodies that way, because it's not small like a virus."

He paused. "On the other hand, it could have been when it first entered their bodies."

"And then grew inside of the body," Teddy added.

So far the conversation was creeping me out, and from the looks on everyone else's face, it was creeping them out too.

"Maybe you two could start at the beginning," Sarah said.

She and Leif were sitting in the corner. At least they were then. I didn't remember seeing them when we first came into the room. When Zeid looked at me with a question on his face, I knew he hadn't seen them either.

Whatever was going to be discussed was important enough for both of them to be present. I didn't see Leif's staff, but I knew it couldn't be far away. Leif saw me looking at him and winked. Not really what some people might expect from a wizard, but it was definitely something Leif would have done in the Earth dimension. He and Sarah were holding hands. Something else they often did in the Earth dimension.

It made me smile, and the thought that they were together again after being in separate dimensions made me think that what was wrong with Erda could be made right. When Sarah smiled and nodded at me, I knew she was thinking the same thing.

But it was hard to hold on to that when Pita and Teddy finally got around to telling us what they had found. It was beyond creepy. It was absolutely terrifying.

Thirty One

After the meeting was over, no one moved. We had been given things to do, but what we had heard was so horrifying it seemed impossible to do anything about it. I knew that given time, we would rally, but at the moment, we were all too stunned to do anything.

Seeing us all sit at the table without moving, Sarah stood and, turning to Niko, said, "Respectively, I think everyone needs to process what they have heard. How about some time off, and then meet later for dinner?"

Niko nodded. He knew no one was going to be able to do anything until we had time to process what we heard. Yes, we had to hurry, but hurrying was not going to work if no one was able to concentrate. I wanted to take the longest hot shower I had ever taken, and I thought I wasn't the only one who wanted to do the same thing.

I had squeezed Zeid's hand, checked to see if the Priscillas in my pocket were doing okay, and gotten up to leave the room when Sarah touched my arm and asked me to walk with her. As we took a few steps down the hall, she peeked into my pocket and saw the Priscillas curled up together, looking miserable. She whispered something, and some of their glow returned. Then Sarah lifted each one out separately, held them gently and whispered something else before they all flew down the hall. They still looked a little wobbly, but much better than they had been a moment before.

"They'll meet you in your room. They'll be okay," Sarah said.

"Really?" I asked. I couldn't suppress the sarcasm in my voice. How could any of us be okay ever again?

Sarah didn't react to my comment. She hooked her arm through mine and pulled me close. It reminded me of the many times in the Earth Realm when Sarah had comforted me, the child. Was I more than a child now? I didn't think so. I wanted to lie down and curl up with my mother and have her tell me that everything was okay.

My mom and I would review our day and tell our secrets to each other. Then she would listen to my prayers while I gave thanks for everyone in my life, and kiss me before turning off the light and softly closing the door.

That's what I wanted. Instead, in Erda, I was no longer a child, and the mother I had here, the Queen, was dead, and I still didn't remember her. Better that way. Then I would be mourning two mothers and two childhoods.

"You can't be a child again, Kara Beth. But you have had the gift of having more than one childhood and more than one loving mother. You gained wisdom and compassion from your time in the Earth dimension. You have the magic and skills from your heritage here in Erda. In one sense, you are the mother now. The mother of the Kingdom of Zerenity."

"I don't feel like that at all, Sarah," I moaned, or whined, depending on your point of view.

Sarah put her arm around me, and I laid my head on her shoulder. We stood that way for a moment, and then Sarah said, "How much do you know about your bracelet?"

She was referring to the bracelet that Link had given me before we went out to fight the Shrieks and Shatterskin. I looked at it on my left arm. It fit as if it had always been there. It was so much a part of me that I rarely thought of it. When I did, I loved the picture-jasper stone set in the center. The veins of the stone formed a tree, and it had been in a beautiful wood box with a tree on it. I kept the box in my room at the Castle.

"Only what Link said to me when he gave it to me. He said he was returning it. But I didn't understand then, and I still don't."

"It's time, then," Sarah said.

She took my hand, and we went into the meditation room where I had first gone to meet with the Oracle. Then it was a little blue light inside of a tree trunk. Later, I realized that the Oracle had been Sarah all along. It made sense to me. She was the wise woman everyone went to back in the Earth Realm. But in Erda, she was more than that. She had restored most of my magic abilities, or at least opened the door for me to find them again.

I knew that there were still some hidden from me.

I hoped that perhaps Sarah would open doors to more of my skills. The thought that I would learn more about the bracelet that I wore got me moving. Instead of shuffling along, I almost flew to the room with her.

The door with the wolf head knocker was there, and I still had to duck to get inside. This time I knew that the different size door was there to make me aware I was entering a different kind of space. If someone walked into the room, as if it was a standard size door, they would whack their head. Needing to duck broke the spell of being unconscious about entering a new place.

Inside, Sarah motioned for me to sit on one of the pads on the floor. It was dark as it had been before. There was still a blue light in a tree trunk, but now Sarah sat opposite me. I realized that she had probably done the same thing the last time that I had been here, I just hadn't seen her.

"Yes, I was here with you, Kara, and I had to let your memory of what happened slowly return. Sometimes our thought processes get in the way of everything. We get caught up in trying to figure things out. Better to listen and let memories and information filter up and become visible in their own time.

"So, you might not remember everything this time, either. But you will in time. When you need it, the information will be there."

I wanted to protest. I needed to know now. I needed to be in control. At the same time, I knew those needs would work against me. What I wanted most was to be whole, and in my heart, my deepest wish was to be part of liberating Erda from Abbadon. Whatever that took, I was willing. Even if it meant I didn't remember everything that happened.

"So you trust me?" Sarah said.

Those words brought back so many memories of things Sarah had done for me and my friends and family in Earth and Erda, that tears started sliding down my face. I couldn't brush them off. Sarah was holding my hands.

"Then you are ready. Let's talk about this bracelet."

Those words were the last thing I remembered.

Thirty Two

The next day we went back to the Castle. We got there using the underground passages instead of walking outside. I wanted to go topside so badly I felt as if I was going to explode with the wanting. It's not that the tunnels and rooms underground are terrible. They aren't. They are warm, cozy, surprisingly clean, and have everything we needed.

What they didn't have was sunshine, breezes, trees, and flowers scenting the air. Usually, this isn't a big deal. No one stayed underground all the time. And we hadn't been underground long either, but with all that was happening it felt as if we had been there for a few years. I had that claustrophobic feeling where everything seems as if it is closing in. I knew I was having that reaction because of what we had learned about Deadsweep, but it didn't change the feeling.

To keep myself from going stir crazy on our walk back, I decided to ask questions about things that had been piling up in my head—unanswered questions. I didn't think any of them pertained directly to Deadsweep, but at least that little corner of my brain where things were that I didn't understand might get tidied up a bit.

My biggest problem was deciding who to ask. Should I move from person to person asking questions, or badger just one? I decided on only one. My first thought was Teddy. But he and the

Ginete brothers were staying in their labs and weren't coming to the Castle with us.

Then I thought of Suzanne. But she had left the tunnels in her dragon persona and was meeting us at the Castle. Sarah and Leif were not around. They were two of the few people in Erda that rarely walked to where they wanted to go. They projected themselves there instead. I had already asked how they did that. How did they appear out of nowhere? But no one would tell me. I was aware that Zeid and Aki could also do that, but I rarely saw them use the skill.

That was one of the questions that I wanted to ask. Why not? If you could project yourself, why walk, or ride a dragon, or maybe a horse? That thought made me wonder. Were there horses in Erda? Why wouldn't there be? How come I had never seen them?

I had a head filled with questions, and I decided that the person who was going to answer them for me was Zeid. He was the one usually walking with me after all, making him easily accessible. Besides, we were betrothed. Shouldn't he be answering questions for me? That was my reasoning.

"Okay, I'll answer most of them, Kara. But I don't guarantee that I will answer all of them. Some I may not even know the answer to. If you agree to those terms, we can begin," Zeid said, coming up beside me.

"Look at that. I didn't even have to call you!" I said. "Turns out I have a great first question. Are you always listening in on my thoughts?"

"Zut. You know better than that, Kara Beth. I have to sleep sometime."

At my sharp intake of breath, he laughed, "Of course not. But your head was boiling over with unanswered questions, so all of your friends decided that it was me who should answer them."

Zeid had gestured behind us to the group that was walking far enough behind us to keep out of trouble. It was evident that they had dropped back to keep me from turning and talking to them.

"Cowards!" I yelled back at them. The Priscillas each gave me an obscene hand gesture which was spoiled by them laughing so hard they almost fell out of the air. "Now, where did they learn that?" I asked Zeid.

"Is that one of your questions?"

"Okay, it is."

"Can't answer. I have no idea. Ask the Priscillas."

By then, I was getting the idea of where this was going to go, but it was still worth a try. Before I began, Zeid held up his hand. "One more thing. I will not answer any questions about us. Those memories will have to come back to you on your own."

"Fair enough," I said. Zeid was right. I was planning to ask him those questions first. I sorted through my questions in my head and decided to ask whatever was up next instead of trying to pick which one was the most important.

"Okay. Why don't you use that projection thing you guys can do more often?"

"I am not as good at it as you might think. For me, it takes up quite a bit of energy, which unless it is necessary, I prefer to save for other things. However, if it is needed, I will do it. Other people find it as easy as walking. I prefer walking. I like to feel the movement."

Zeid finished and looked at me expectantly.

"Okay, here's another. Remember after one of the battles with the Shrieks, I was told that Ruta traveled by tree? No one ever told me what that meant."

Zeid turned around and looked back at Ruta, who gave me a look which I guess Zeid knew to be a yes because he answered me. "Ruta is related to trees."

That didn't surprise me. Ruta always reminded me of a block of wood with elf-like qualities. But that raised even more questions. I left those questions alone and asked again, "But how does he travel by tree?"

"He steps into the tree and goes with the flow. The flow could go up, or across the forest tree to tree, or down into the roots."

"What? How can he do that? Does he melt into the tree?"

"Kind of like that. But I don't know more about how. And if you are going to ask how Ruta became a healer, or anything about his past, or family, that is for him to answer."

"Okay. Here's a simple one. When I first came to the Castle, Earl and Suzanne were talking about the metal toadstools not being on the grid. What grid?"

"You're right, that's an easy one. They were talking about the communication systems that we use. The metal toadstools, as you call them, can't tap into those systems. That's because we worry that Abbadon might make use of them. As you know, he seems to have a way with machines."

I nodded—that made sense. "Now I have one I can't work out at all. I was gone only two years from Erda, but I remembered two lifetimes (although short ones) in the Earth dimension. How do people travel through the portals when they would keep ending up going backward or forwards?

"For example, if I ever got to revisit my Earth home, everyone would be much, much, older. I don't get it. When Suzanne or Leif visited, it was the same time in both places when they returned."

While I was talking, I could feel Zeid tensing up. When I was done asking the question, he turned to Niko who was now right behind us and said, "Not one I can answer. This question is all yours."

Niko smiled and came up beside us and said. "It's tricky. The portal adjusts the time."

"Every portal adjusts the time?" I asked.

"As far as we know," Niko answered. "And yes, if the timing didn't work that would be a bit of a mess, wouldn't it?"

For the rest of the walk we were all silent. Niko hadn't really answered my question. And something about portals and time was nagging at me, but I didn't have the question yet, let alone the answer.

Actually, that was the problem with everything going on with Deadsweep. We didn't know the question yet. Maybe we should start there.

THIRTY THREE

On the surface, everything at the Castle looked pretty much the same as it did before we left. Before we discovered the horrible things going on in Dalry.

The Castle is so big nothing changed when all the Castle staff and their families were brought inside. Once everyone was in, the doors were shut until further notice. That was one reason we arrived through the underground tunnels. The outside doors were bolted.

Until we popped up in the atrium, I didn't even know there was an entrance to the tunnels in the Castle. It was probably one of the many secrets hidden within those Castle walls.

I didn't know who arranged it so that we popped up inside the atrium, but I sent them a blast of gratitude. I suspected it was Teddy's doing.

Being in the atrium was almost as delightful as being outside. The sides of the atrium were four stories high and was filled with trees and flowers. The atrium was so beautiful I laughed out loud with happiness. Although the glass ceiling was closed, the sun was streaming in through the glass and felt warm and soft on my face.

I remembered the first time I saw the atrium's garden. It had reminded me of Sarah's garden in the Earth Realm. It still did, and I wondered if perhaps Sarah had a hand in its creation.

It was lunchtime by the time we arrived. The table was loaded with food. The metal toadstools stood by as always to bring us more if we wanted it. Although everything looked the same, the atmosphere in the Castle had changed. I knew everyone felt it. But we all ignored it as we sat around the table laughing and enjoying each other.

We were buying time, just as the walk to the Castle had bought us time. Every one of us needed time to think about what Pita and Teddy had told us and what it meant.

Plus, we needed to rest. Based on what we had heard, we were going to have some traveling to do. But first we needed a plan, and that's what we didn't have.

After lunch, everyone went their separate ways. We were to meet in a few hours in Professor Link's classroom. It was the same room where he had tried to teach me magic. I guess he showed me something because I had some magic skills now. At least I had more magic skills than I had a few months ago.

But I knew what Link would say. He would say that I didn't get them—I remembered them. He would add that the need to remember was true for everyone. You didn't get your skills. You had them. And then sometimes forgot them, or ignored them, or put them down as not useful or not spectacular enough.

Link told me that the labeling of skills, making one more important than another, is dangerous. Well, Link says it's idiotic, which kind of sounds like labeling to me, but I know what he means.

This is the man who can step into a fire and then pull flames out and use it to light the herbs in a ceremonial bowl. When I once talked to the Professor about the time I saw him do that and remarked how awesome it was, he made a face like something was stinky and slapped that idea down immediately.

"What about the person who cooks your meals, Kara Beth? Or plants the flowers you love and helps them thrive? Or built the houses we stay in? Or the stone smith, the storyteller, or the person who takes care of the sick?

"These skills may not be flashy, but we need them. Wishing you could step into a fire without being burned is wishing for an illusion. It means nothing. Wish to be of service. Know that what is needed at the moment is something you can provide. Perhaps it is a flame, but just as important it might be a bowl of food or a song."

I had stayed in the garden while I waited for the meeting thinking about that, and that's where Professor Link found me.

"So you are thinking about the conversation about magic and skills?" he asked.

"I am. I'm also thinking about what Suzanne said as we were preparing our plan to stop the Shrieks and Shatterskin. She reminded us that it is the community that will defeat Abbadon. Not just one person. She was right. When we stopped the Shrieks and Shatterskin, it was all of us doing what we do best, but not by ourselves.

"I am beginning to see how it is impossible to do anything on our own. Everything, literally everything, is connected. How can Abbadon not see that?"

Link squinted at me. I used to be afraid of that squint. Maybe I still was, but now I knew that sometimes the squint was a good thing. "Kara, I think he does know that everything is connected, but doesn't like it. It's part of his driving force to rip that connection apart.

"The fact that the infection he is sending across the planet does rip friends and families apart is delightful to him. He can get us to attack each other, while he sits back in his version of a Castle and gloats. I think he is trying to prove to himself that connection is what is evil and not him."

There wasn't anything I could say about that. It was inconceivable to me that someone could believe such a thing, and then make it his life's mission to destroy connection and then all life forms. It would leave him on a dead planet. What good would that do? Abbadon uses his victims as sources of power. Once he depletes them, they die. Sooner or later, there would be no one left. Had he not thought this through? He would die too without life around him."

"Perhaps he thinks he can reinvent life," Link said.

I looked at Link in bewilderment. But there was nothing to say. What if he could? Was it possible?

Link and I sat in the garden together watching the butterflies and bees move from flower to flower. They were a beautiful symbol of our interconnection and need for each other. If Abbadon thought he could reproduce that, he was delusional. But then we all knew that he was. The question was, how do you stop a crazy person?

Link answered my unspoken question. "In Abbadon's case by stopping his latest monster, Deadsweep. Then we will go after him."

I nodded at Link and then lay back onto the mossy ground, felt the breath of the earth moving through me, and fell asleep.

When I woke, Link was gone, and I was refreshed and ready. I knew there was a solution, and I knew we would find it. We had to. There was no room for failure.

THIRTY FOUR

The Priscillas were waiting for me in my room when I stopped in to splash water on my face in preparation for the meeting. I hadn't seen them all day. Usually, they were hanging in my pocket or riding in Cahir's fur. Come to think of it; I had no idea where Cahir was, either. Or Beru. I had been so caught up in the Deadsweep problem I hadn't realized they were missing.

What was wrong with me? How could I not have noticed that my friends were not around me as they usually were? It was a rift in my thinking. Maybe that was how the infection began. It made you forget your friends?

The idea that perhaps I was already infected with Abbadon's Deadsweep made me feel like throwing up. I tried to sit down on the bed and missed, ending up on the floor. In the middle of being upset about Deadsweep, instead of doing something useful, I was as clumsy as ever.

Maybe someday I wouldn't be as awkward. Maybe. On the other hand, perhaps I would be known as the Clumsy Princess. The one who no longer lived because she died in the Deadsweep epidemic.

Usually, my clumsiness would cause the Priscillas to break out into their tinkling bell laughter. This time they barely smiled.

"Ziffer. I am infected, aren't I? That's why I haven't seen you, and you look so miserable. Did the Whistle Pigs prepare another jail room? You better put me in jail right now, before it gets worse."

"Oh, for Pete's sake, Kara, snap out of it," Pris said. "You're not infected with anything other than human idiocy. Some days you display worse stupidity than others. Perhaps you'll grow out of it. But right now, you are acting ridiculous. Everything is not all about you."

"Oh. An idiot. No big deal," I said as I picked myself up and sat on the bed. I noticed that Pris didn't pull my hair to emphasize her point. That too, was unusual.

"What's going on? Why are the three of you so glum? Your wings aren't even sparkling."

I gathered the three of them and put them in my lap where they sat looking like Tinkerbell when no one believed in her. I didn't think that clapping my hands together was going to help them.

"What can I do?"

They just sat there shaking their heads, wings drooping. Pris was even missing a bow from her pigtails.

"Okay, you don't have to talk, but you are coming with me to the meeting."

Tucking the three of them in the crook of my arm, I stooped to pick up the tiny bow I had spotted on the floor. I put that in my pocket. I knew Pris would perk up soon. The three of them were some of the happiest beings I had ever met. They were courageous and loyal. Whatever was bothering them would not keep them down, and Pris would want to be looking perfect when we headed off to stop the Deadsweep.

The atmosphere in Link's classroom was almost as downbeat as the Priscilla's mood. Almost. Because standing at the front of the room was Pita looking as upbeat as he had ever looked.

That's not to say that knowing how a Ginete is feeling is an easy tell. But his eyes were a bright gold, and he winked at me when I came in the room, causing me to stumble over a chair.

Had Pita ever winked at me? Do Ginete wink? Did I imagine it? I straightened up and headed to my seat amidst titters of laughter over my stumble. Didn't I say I would be known as the Clumsy Princess?

In the middle of the stumble, I looked at Pita's face again. Yep. He winked at me. I wasn't sure if anyone else had noticed. However, the laughter at my expense did seem to have lightened up the mood a bit.

If that is what it took to brighten people's days, I could stumble around all the time. I could include it as one of my magical skills.

I sat in the empty chair beside Beru. She reached over and slid her hand across the top of mine, and we wiggled our fingers at each other, reminding me once again how much she meant to me. If I had a sister, I would have wanted her to be just like Beru.

Beru leaned over and whispered, "Me, too."

"Well, then," I whispered back, "Love you, sis."

We laughed together, and although a few faces turned to look at us, they weren't angry at our laughing. They were curious about what could be joyful in the middle of this crisis, and they wanted in on it. Beru and I wiggled our fingers at everyone, and a few smiles broke out.

Zeid slid into the seat beside me and whispered, "That's my girl. Sparking joy. I'll take that in a Clumsy Princess any day."

The face I turned towards him must have been beaming, because a bolt of happiness had shot up inside of me so hard that I almost levitated out of my chair. I was Zeid's girl. Sure, I had been told that I was. But this time I felt it. He chose me.

Pita cleared his throat to get our attention. He was standing on a platform so that we could all see him.

"I know some of you are wondering why I am here since I had stayed behind to get some answers. I know you are hoping that I have some."

"Do you?" John asked. "I know we are ready for some. So if you do, could you get on with it? All I can think about is what you told us last time. It's not an infection in the same way that a virus is an infection. That was good news. But what you told us was even scarier. So, are you planning to scare us again and have no answers?"

Although John's way of speaking was often harsh, he brought up things people were thinking, so a wave of agreement went around the room. It didn't faze Pita at all. Instead, he waited until it passed and then Pita said, "We have more answers. And we have some ideas on how to stop it. How does that sound to you?"

He glanced over at me, and I winked at him. Now I understood the message.

THIRTY FIVE

Pita had hope. That's what I knew Pita was telling me. And he wanted me to support his message.

Once he had everyone's attention, Pita began his story. The Ginete and the Whistle Pigs had an idea they thought would work. First Pita went over what they had discovered the day before while Zeid and I had been in the village talking to the dead man's family.

Using the suits, breathers, and goggles as protection, they had taken samples from all three men. None of them showed a viral infection, which led them back to what in the Earth dimension might have been called a mental illness.

What made this different is that they knew that this mental illness was something that Abbadon had caused. It had turned three loving and happy men into what we had seen. They became killers, almost overnight.

But how did they become infected? The answer was so creepy that all of us had nightmares since Pita had shown us. They had discovered the culprit by accident.

The body of the dead man had been left in the sub-zero room to preserve it until they knew more. The morning Zeid and I were in the village, Pita had just happened to glance in the window to the room, and saw something crawl out of the dead man's ear.

It was lucky timing, because if Pita hadn't seen it crawl out, it might have disappeared forever. Pita captured it and then he and

Teddy studied it. They concluded that the little worm had been living in the man's brain and had probably done all that damage.

Just hearing Pita talk about it again made my skin crawl. Pita had brought along the worm inside of a bottle. It was about an inch long and looked like an ordinary earthworm. Except on closer inspection, the skin was rubber, and there was a tiny red spot on the top of his head.

Perhaps Abbadon made them with the red dots so he could easily tell the difference between his worms and a regular worm.

"Ear-worms are what people call those songs that get stuck in your head, so a thought-worm is the perfect name for these worms. They live in your head, and they manipulate your thoughts," Pita said.

Pita opened the jar and held the worm in his hand. Even though we knew it was dead, we all had a moment of fear. The idea that the thing would crawl into your ear and make you crazy was terrifying.

But this worm was most definitely dead. Not that it had ever been alive, because as creepy as a real worm in your ear might be, this worm beat that.

Pita laid the worm down and then lifted the top half of its body off. Inside was a tiny computer.

"This is what makes this worm work." Pita pointed to a small round thing near the top of its head, and said, "This is how it sees where it is going.

"We think that once it gets inside someone's head, it is programmed so well it finds the nerves and amygdala that control thinking and start messing with them using various signals.

"It also appears to have the ability to manipulate the thyroid gland, which begins to upset the balance of emotions. The body becomes flooded with hormones and testosterone, and everything goes crazy.

"Even though we usually don't think of ourselves as a machine, our bodies do function like one. We aren't consciously running it, but its functions are easily disrupted."

Niko stepped in and said, "It makes sense that Abbadon would once again try to disrupt the body. First, he used sound waves. Now he is more refined.

"He has found something that directly upsets the body's system. No more noise necessary. Can't see this little bugger coming. Makes it so much harder to destroy. We might have thought that the Shrieks and Shatterskin were hard, but at least we knew where they were.

"Once he realized that we had figured out how to disrupt his machines, he built something small enough and unexpected enough to be silently effective. But he is still using devices. This time, though, his machines are causing people to go after each other. He just sets the destruction in motion, and then enjoys the result.

"I don't think he believed we would figure this out this quickly. If the body had not been in that room, and the room hadn't been that cold, and Pita wouldn't have looked in the window at that time, we would still not know.

"We don't think it occurred to him that we would freeze a body. That's most likely why he waited until warmer weather. Plus, he probably figured everyone would be too afraid to get near each other, especially those that were infected. That meant the worm would remain undetected, maybe forever."

"So you are saying that the worm would usually stay inside of a dead body? Wouldn't they want that worm to crawl back out and infect someone else?" Zeid asked.

"We don't think so," Pita answered. "This worm doesn't appear to have a working signal anymore. We think it 'dies' when its host dies. We think Abbadon was more interested in keeping it a secret than infecting someone else. Besides, he can probably manufacture as many as he wants.

"Abbadon likes machines. He knows how they work, and probably does see the body as nothing more than a machine. It would answer the question as to why he finds it so easy to kill."

"But then, wouldn't he see himself as a machine?" I asked.

"It's very possible that he does. And that is why he doesn't need anything else to live. If he can design machines that keep his machine—his body—running, then he might be perfectly happy. I wouldn't be surprised if that's on his bucket list," Niko answered.

We all snickered. A bucket list with two things on it: kill every living thing and find a way to live forever—alone.

After the laughter died down, Niko said. "Since we think we might have the upper hand here because now we know what is causing this mental illness, and Abbadon doesn't know that we know, this information cannot leave our team. For any reason.

"We can't talk about it in the atrium or the halls. Pick one of the safe rooms to speak together, or don't talk about this at all. We have no idea if Abbadon has ways of finding out what we know."

"At one point, you thought perhaps we had a traitor among us. Do you still think so?" I asked. It might have been a pretty dumb question to ask, but I needed to know.

Professor Link answered my question. "No. Not in this room. Not with the Ginete, or the Whistle Pigs that we are working with. Otherwise, we would not be having this meeting. But somehow Abbadon finds things out. We don't know how. I will be switching channels to speak with you often. I'll find you, though, so don't panic."

"Okay," John said. We all smiled. Here goes John, asking the question we all wanted to know.

"I see you clarified a few things. And those zonking worms are disgusting. But is there a plan, or not, to get rid of this invasion of Deadsweep?"

"There is," Pita said.

THIRTY SIX

"Let me get this straight," John said. No one missed his sarcastic tone of voice. "You have figured out how to stop these disgusting thought-worms from crawling into people's ears and making them crazy?

"Really? How are we supposed to do that? We don't know where they come from. We don't have a clue how they choose who to infect. Is it targeted, or is it random?

"We don't know ziffer. At least we don't, but you do? Are you guys some kind of freaks or what? Or are you holding out on us, so you have all the control? Maybe you guys make the thought-worms and are blaming it on Abbadon."

James put a comforting hand on John's shoulder, but John shook it off and turned to glare at him and the other three men in the village.

We had all seen John upset, but had we seen him this upset before? Then I had a terrible thought. I started wondering if he was angrier than necessary. Was he irrational? Was he infected? If he was, was anyone else?

Everyone else must have had a version of the same thought because the room became deadly silent. John looked at everyone staring at him and stood up so quickly his chair fell over.

"Oh, zut no. You're not going to say I'm infected. I'm rational, while you all are delusional."

When no one said anything in response, John turned to Pita, who was still standing on the platform at the front of the room and said, "Please tell me that I am not infected."

Pita smiled at him and said, "John, your questions are valid, and we'll go through them together. I'll tell you what we have answers to and what we don't. And yes, we do have the beginnings of a plan for moving forward.

"As I said, we have the upper hand. It's doubtful that Abbadon knows we understand how Deadsweep works. It's obvious the first thing to do is to keep him in the dark as long as possible.

"As far as you being infected, I have good news for you. We have a way to find out. In fact, Teddy has set up a room for everyone to be checked."

The room erupted as we all realized what he had said. Some of us might be infected, but instead of it being a mystery until we violently acted out, we could now tell.

Pita held up his hand. "That's the good news. The bad news? We don't know how to get the worm out without freezing your brain. Obviously, that's not the answer. But we can isolate you until we find a 'cure.'"

Niko stood. "Perhaps the best thing to do is have everyone checked before we continue this meeting. That way, anyone can disagree without everyone else worrying that they are infected. I'll get us started. I'll go first."

A murmur of agreement went around the room. Teddy must have been waiting outside the door for Pita to let us know about the testing because as Niko said those words, Teddy came into the room.

He looked exhausted. No wonder. The Ginete and Whistle Pigs had been working nonstop, and then they still had to travel to the Castle and set up while the rest of us ate and slept.

I raised my hand. I hadn't been brought up in Earth schools for nothing. At Pita's nod, I asked, "What about other beings? Are they infected the same way? Like the birds and animals? And ..." my voice faltered as I looked down at the Priscillas hiding in my pocket.

Niko reassured me. "As far as we know, birds and animals are not infected. There would have to be very tiny worms and specially designed for their brains. I am not saying that Abbadon hasn't thought of this, or will. And we don't know how it would affect different beings. Perhaps they wouldn't be angry; maybe something else would happen."

I stood there trying not to give away what I was afraid of, but Beru understood immediately and said, "May Kara Beth go first and take her friends in with her?"

The light dawned on Teddy, and he put his arm around me. "I'll take Flower Girl and Miss Princess and her friends with me first. Then perhaps you could all file in one at a time after that."

"One more thing," Niko said. "What happens if one of us is infected? Will we voluntarily go to be locked away until the cure is found? Or is there something in place to help us make that decision?"

The horror of what Niko was saying hit everyone at once. We might have to establish some kind of police force—unheard of in Erda. The police in Erda did things like rescue animals out of trees. They never used force or detained a criminal. Criminals hadn't existed before in Erda. Well, other than the master criminal, Abbadon.

Having come from the Earth Realm and witnessing what could happen when any group gains that kind of power, even with the best intentions in the world, fear ran down my spine.

Deadsweep was a brilliant move on Abbadon's part. He could systemically destroy the Kingdom of Zerenity without any danger to himself. We would become the danger. One infected person in charge and everything went to hell in a hand basket, as my father used to say jokingly.

I knew how fast evil could spread this way. It could quickly reach a tipping point that we could never turn back from. I wasn't sure that the people in the room understood how deadly dangerous Deadsweep could be within a very short period of time.

Suzanne looked at me across the room. She knew. She had traveled to Earth. She had seen how quickly retribution, revenge, control, and greed could spread. Once another creature was perceived as not as important, or different, it was possible to kill them or destroy their life without remorse.

Erda was not prepared for this. They wouldn't know what had happened to them.

I stood by the door, paralyzed by the fear of what could happen. It was Suzanne that broke the spell by reminding me of something I had heard over and over again in the Earth dimension—heard and seen proven time and time again.

"Good is always stronger than evil, Hannah," Suzanne said.

She wanted me to remember what Hannah knew, and Kara Beth had to live by, too.

"So say we all," I said.

"So say we all," responded everyone in the room, including John. We were going to be okay.

THIRTY SEVEN

"Why did you set this room up in the Castle, Teddy," I asked as we walked. "Why not leave us all down under and set it up there?"

"We do have one set up—down under, as you call it—however, we need some here too." He nodded at one of the people working in the Castle, and I understood.

"You need to check everyone, don't you?"

"We do. We need to know there is no one in trouble here. The Castle must be a completely safe space. Once the team leaves, we will be bringing more people into the Castle. But first, we need to make sure they are not ill. If they are, we'll isolate them.

"We have already checked all the Ginete and Whistle Pigs that work with you. Not sure those thought-worms will work on us, but of course we have to check, anyway."

By then we had reached the room where the Whistle Pigs had set up a testing room. It was odd seeing so many Whistle Pigs in the Castle. Usually, they were off in the tunnels working on one thing or another. I smiled at them all, and they waved their massive hands in response. I was proud of myself. I was beginning to be able to tell them apart.

"Don't worry, Princess Pea," Teddy whispered, "We had trouble telling you guys apart, too, at first."

We both broke into giggles. I don't know if the other Whistle Pigs could read our thoughts, but our giggles made them giggle too. Soon the whole room was laughing over nothing, really. But it sure felt good and broke the spell of gloom that had been hovering over the place.

The room they used was just another of the many beautiful places in the Castle. Now it had been set up with six stations partitioned off from each other with colorful curtains.

"Thank you for making this cheerful, Teddy," I said.

"Speaking of cheerful," Teddy whispered, nodding at my pocket.

I looked at him with a pleading look. He knew what I was asking. Would the test be okay for the Priscillas? And did he know what was wrong with them?

"It will, and I don't," he whispered into my ear, "But don't worry. Let's do this first."

A Whistle Pig came over and led Beru to one of the curtained stations, and Teddy took me to mine.

"This is like a cross between an X-Ray and an MRI. However, it won't make noise, and the rays that are going to look into your head aren't dangerous. But the Priscillas would be better off doing this in the space that we have for those that are not so 'human.'"

I lifted the Priscillas out of my pocket and placed them gently in Teddy's hands, and he took them over to another station. I lay down on the bed, and a small drone like thing briefly hovered over my head and then moved away.

"Okay, all done," Teddy said handing the Priscillas back to me. I kissed the top of their heads and noticed they were a little perkier. I thought it was probably that their curiosity had been piqued. Fairies are like me. They like knowing everything.

"That's it? Do you have the results?"

Teddy took me by the elbow and led me out to a row of tables on the other side of the room. Beru was already there waiting for me. The other four Ginete brothers were staffing the tables. There was what looked like a laptop in front of each of them.

The Ginete I knew as Sam turned the machine around and I saw a picture of what I knew to be a brain.

"Your brain," Sam said. "Nothing there, and nothing in Beru's or the Priscillas, either."

We all laughed. Nothing in my brain sounded about right.

By then everyone had arrived ready to be tested. The line going in was sober and understandably withdrawn. The line coming out was noticeably cheerier.

I noticed Ruta standing on the side looking miserable. I knew he was in charge of taking people away if they were infected. The reasoning was he was the most unlikely of everyone to be infected by either the thought-worms or the desire to be in command.

They were right about that. Ruta was incorrigible. He might be Mr. Grouch, he might not always approve of me, but Ruta was, well, Ruta was Ruta. I considered it one of the blessings of coming to Erda to have met Ruta. I waved at him. He pretended not to see me, but I saw the hint of a smile on his face. I wanted to hug him, but he would have hated that, so I just winked at him.

We had agreed to meet in the atrium for dinner after the testing was done. The table was already set when we arrived. We sat down, and the metal toadstools came by with their trays of food. I was starving. I hadn't realized how afraid I had been that I was infected. Now that that worry had been taken away, I felt a million times better.

Everyone else must have experienced the same thing because as another person entered the room, everyone brightened up more and more. James walked in with his brother John who looked the happiest I had ever seen him. I couldn't stop myself. I hopped up and ran over to John and hugged him.

"Thank you, Kara," John whispered in my ear. "I am not sure I deserve your admiration. I'm so negative sometimes."

I stepped back and held John's hands and said, "We need you to question John. Don't stop asking things that we might have missed."

James leaned over and kissed my cheek. I hugged him as he said, "Thank you, Hannah." I loved that James treated me like a daughter. His daughter Liza was a lucky girl.

When Ruta walked in as light-hearted as I had ever seen him, we knew all was well. No one in the Castle was infected with Deadsweep. Even the Priscillas were back to being mischievous. They flew over to Ruta and sat on his head. To his credit, he didn't flinch.

Niko stood at the front of the table, holding up his glass of water. I used to think of him like a gazelle on steroids. He used to scare me. Now, I was so used to him, I had forgotten how much he looked like a Greek statue. His dark skin glowed in the light coming down through the atrium ceiling.

Niko taught us how to fight if necessary, but this fight was going to be different, and we all knew it. So he was standing there to encourage us all. We had passed the first test. There was more to come, but at that moment we were reveling in our good fortune.

"To us," Niko said.

"To us," we responded.

THIRTY EIGHT

"These are the things we need to work out," Niko said.

We were back in Professor Link's classroom after having dinner.

"We have some ideas for each area, but let's see if we can fill in more gaps by stating the problems up front.

"Here's what we know. We know why people are acting out. The thought-worms are causing brains to malfunction. We know the worms live inside the brain. We know that in subzero cold they crawl out of the person's ear and die. We know how to determine if someone is infected.

"Here's what we don't know. We conjecture that even though the thought-worms enter through the ear, it's possible they get in another way too.

"We don't know how Abbadon is getting them here. What's the mode of delivery? How come some people are infected, and others aren't? We don't know how to kill them. We don't know how to get them out of an infected person, without killing the person."

Niko paused and looked around the room. None of us moved. It sounded hopeless. How were we supposed to stop something we knew so little about?

"Well, what was the big plan that Pita mentioned?" John asked, almost as sarcastically as he had been earlier that day.

"I think you have seen the results of what the Ginete and Whistle Pigs have accomplished so far, John. Without them, we wouldn't know anything at all. We wouldn't know that the thought-worms existed, nor would we be able to test people to be sure they are safe.

"While they were finding all that out, what were we doing? We were waiting for the information. We need to give Pita and Teddy our thanks, not our scorn.

"And to make that more imperative, we believe that it is possible that rifts between people, or within themselves, make us more attractive to the thought-worms. Easier to manipulate. Therefore, I stress that we remain calm and supportive of everyone, at all times.

"You can see that the Ginete are not here," Niko continued. "That's because they are busy preparing the next phase. They have not stopped working on the way to destroy Deadsweep before it's too late."

"What is the next phase?" I asked, sparing John the embarrassment of being the only one who asked the questions. Besides, I could see that he was still seething over Niko's response. However, I knew Niko was right. We needed to heal all rifts. I trusted that his brother, James, would help John. I thought John was so scared he didn't know what else to do but act out.

Niko's face hardened as he answered my question. "Tomorrow morning most of us will be leaving the Castle. After being tested, more people will be let into the Castle. Then the doors will be closed again.

"A few Whistle Pigs will stay to maintain drone stations. They will need them just in case they need to test someone in the Castle. This decision is more for peace of mind than the belief that someone here will be infected later.

"Since we don't know how Deadsweep thought-worms are transmitted, everything that comes into the Castle will be monitored. There won't be much to track because the Castle is self-contained. Little, if anything, will be coming in. However, if something shows up, all of us will be alerted.

"In the meantime, some of us are heading back to Dalry to try and determine what the three men had in common."

Niko paused and looked towards Suzanne.

"Thank you, Niko," Suzanne said, taking over. "The dragons have brought bad news. Terrible news. There is unrest in every village that they have flown over."

"Which means every village is infected?" John shouted.

"It means that in all the villages that they have seen, someone is infected. We can see the results of the fighting, and people are staying out of their gardens and the streets."

Beru and the four men from their village stood up together. "Our village?" Beru asked for them all.

"Yes, we saw evidence of violence in Kinver, which is why the five of you and a Whistle Pig will be returning to Kinver in a Sound Bubble tomorrow. We'll be sending you with the drone that can check people, so you can isolate those that are infected from those that aren't."

"We can't send people everywhere, so we are concentrating on just a few villages. Kinver, Dalry, and Eiddwen. Dragons will be watching over each town, and there will be a drone for each group.

"Eiddwen was closed down the minute you left, Kara Beth. So far there is no sign of the infection, but we are in touch with Berta at all times, and she will let us know at the first sign. I sent a dragon to her yesterday with the drone and earplugs.

"Oh yes, earplugs. Although the thought-worms may be entering through other places than the ears, we do have a fairly invisible plug for everyone to wear in your ears. It's almost the same technology as the ear muffs had been. You will hear just fine, but nothing can get inside your ears."

"What if it's not through the ears?" I asked.

"That's why no one sleeps alone. We would notice if something crawled on us while we are awake. So while you sleep, someone else is going to be watching you at all times."

When Suzanne said that Eiddwen was safe, at least for now, I had collapsed back on my seat. I hadn't realized how frightened I had been that my father and all the lovely people I had met were in danger, or infected. It was such a relief I almost didn't hear Suzanne say Berta's name. It took a beat before I realized what she said.

"So Berta has been in touch with you all this time? Even while I was there?"

"Of course," Suzanne laughed. "Do you think we would have left you undefended or us out of touch for even a minute?"

If things weren't such a mess, I probably would have indulged a moment of pouting, but I managed to collect myself and act more like a grownup before anyone noticed except for Zeid who gave a soft snort. I tried one of Beru's looks on him, but that only made him snort again.

Niko stepped to the front of the room again. "What we haven't talked about yet is how we are going to subdue the villagers fighting each other. We have to do it without hurting anyone. And we will have to contain them. And feed them. And hope they don't die before we discover how to get the thought-worms out."

"How big a problem is this?" Zeid asked.

"In Dalry, almost everyone is fighting each other. There are only a few pockets where people are hiding from their own family and friends. It's bad. In the few days we have been gone, something happened. We need to find out what and how as quickly as possible.

"The enemy that we will be fighting are our own people. Just as Abbadon wanted it to be."

THIRTY NINE

The sun was just coming up over the horizon, a few rays hitting the top floors of the atrium. We were all waiting for the Sound Bubble. James, John, Thomas, and Mark stood together, James with his arm around John's shoulder. They looked frightened, but determined.

Beru was with me. We had stepped behind one of the enormous ferns, and I was sobbing. Beru was doing her best to comfort me, but she was torn between leaving me and knowing she had to go to Kinver.

The people in Kinver had not listened to her when she had told them about the Shrieks and Shatterskin. Later, the villagers had learned that she was right and stepped up to help fight. Beru hoped that they would listen to her and the brothers now as they attempted to protect the villagers against themselves.

If there were only a few infected people in the town, Beru and the men going back with her would use the other townspeople's help to isolate the infected ones, and then use the gas that the Ginete had prepared to keep them subdued until we could find a cure.

If Kinver was engulfed with violence, the only choice they had was to get the ones who were not yet infected back to the relative safety of the Castle, using the Sound Bubbles.

"Don't cry, Kara Beth," Beru said, "We'll be fine. It won't be long before we meet again. Besides, we'll be able to talk all the time on the channels that Professor Link has set up."

I nodded and hugged her close, and she let me, resting her head on my shoulder. A few moments later, we heard the beautiful harmony of the Sound Bubble coming closer. We walked hand in hand out to join everyone else and then, wiggling her fingers at me, Beru went to stand with the men and a Whistle Pig named Pete. Pete carried a bag which I knew contained the drone and the gas. I had already sobbed on James' shoulder. He too, had promised me that he and his family would be safe.

The glass ceiling opened, and the bubble slowly descended. It is hard to feel anything but joy when the Sound Bubble arrives. It lowered itself and surrounded all six of them within seconds, paused, and lifted off. I waved until the bubble had risen out of sight and the ceiling had closed. I didn't care that tears were still streaming down my face. I had learned that tears were a good thing, and just because I had tears on my face didn't mean that I wasn't ready.

The next to leave were Suzanne and Aki. They were going to Eiddwen. I hugged them both goodbye, not stopping to think that Aki had never hugged me before. I knew Aki had skills I had not yet experienced. I knew she could take care of herself. But I needed her to know how much she meant to me, so I had hugged her as hard as I could.

Aki was riding Suzanne, as Lady the dragon, to Eiddwen to assist Berta with the village. The first thing they were going to do was test my father, King Darius. If he were free of the Deadsweep, they would put him into a Sound Bubble and return him to the Castle. That was the plan. He wasn't going to be given a chance to say no.

There was a side benefit. Perhaps being in the Castle with his people would rouse my father from the depression he had fallen into. Leif had said he would help, and I had a feeling a little wizard magic might be just what my father needed.

Leif and Sarah had appeared in time to say goodbye to everyone. They were staying in the Castle with Link. Link needed to be safe to keep all our channels open. Leif and Sarah could be wherever they were required at any moment, but staying in the Castle meant they could help with the crowds of people who would be arriving, and help keep order. And of course, support the Ginete and Whistle Pigs who were staying behind. They would be using the information that we would send back to find the answers to all the questions we still had.

We still needed to know how the thought-worms were getting from town to town. We needed to know how to stop them from entering the brain and how to remove them from everyone that has already been infected.

The teams going out into the towns would be doing crowd control and information gathering, but it was the people back in the Castle who were going to discover how to stop Deadsweep from taking over the Kingdom of Zerenity.

Suzanne stepped into a clearing in the atrium and transformed into Lady. It never failed to amaze me. One second she was the beautiful Suzanne, and the next she was a beautiful pileated dragon. She was still Suzanne, but also Lady the dragon. A dragon that had grown big enough to carry a person, or two, or three.

Aki climbed onto Lady's back. Aki carried a drone and the gas in a backpack. Link wanted to send a Whistle Pig with them, but Aki said they would be fine. And, besides, a Whistle Pig riding a dragon wasn't going to happen. Both Lady and the Whistle Pig agreed with that decision.

Aki's eyes grew dark, the ceiling opened, and they were off. Watching them leave, I remembered that Suzanne had hinted there were other shapeshifters in Erda, and I wondered if I would meet them soon.

Beside me, I heard Professor Link whisper, "God speed." I had a feeling that he was directing that wish to Aki more than anyone else, and I wondered if there was something more going on between the two of them than just friendship.

If Beru had been there, she would have pinched my leg to make sure I didn't say anything. Instead, this time it was Zeid who pinched me, which startled me so much I jumped a little, but no one seemed to notice. Everyone had too many tears in their eyes to see anything.

FORTY

After everyone had gone, those of us who were left had one last meeting with Link. Niko, Zeid, Ruta, and I were going to Dalry. It was where the dragons had reported the most violence, and Link wanted to go over a few things with us before we headed out.

He reminded us that our main job was to find a connection between the three men, and to extract the remaining unaffected people from the village without getting hurt ourselves, or harming anyone.

There was one more thing that I was supposed to do. I was to try out using my bracelet. Sarah had shown me what my mother used to do with it, but there had been no time to practice.

Everyone going to Dalry had seen the bracelet in action when my mother used it. Why she didn't have it on her when she went to visit Ruta's village no one would ever know. However, I knew that everyone assumed she wanted to make sure her daughter, me, had it in case she never came back.

Mom had given it to Link right after they sent me to the Earth dimension. She had asked him to give it to me as soon as I returned to Erda. At the time, no one knew I would forget all my magic skills and would have to rediscover them. I think my mother thought I would put it on, and boom, I would be able to help save the Kingdom with it. After all, I was her daughter. It didn't happen.

Once Sarah realized that I needed help to access what it could do and that I was ready to learn, she stepped in to teach me. Sarah projected pictures of my mother practicing with the bracelet. Like the skills that Niko taught, no one thought about using magic as a defense or as a weapon until Abbadon decided to take over the world. Watching my Erda mother, Rowena, practice, I knew she had been practicing for fun, with no thought it would be necessary for defending anything.

Knowing I would never see her again, and that her final wishes were for me to be happy and safe, was hard for me. Watching her had been both devastating and exciting. It was in her memory that I would use the bracelet. And like her, only for good.

The jasper stone's picture in the bracelet depicted a tree, and it was the powers of trees and stones that I was going to call upon. Picture jasper is valued for its deep connection to the earth. After all, it was the pressures and the forces of the planet that formed the picture found in the stone.

The stone itself symbolizes nurturing and protection, while the tree is the provider of all the things that life needs in Erda. The two of them together plus what Sarah was teaching me, would be very helpful during our mission to Dalry. That is, if I could make it work.

If all else failed, I could shoot lightning bolts and fireballs, but I wasn't sure either of those would be useful except for maybe as scare tactics to get people to listen. I didn't think that the thought-worms were going to turn and run away from me because of the lightning display. Although I did love the picture of those little worms slithering as fast as possible to their destruction.

Link also reminded me of the button that I wore. If I was in trouble, I was to push it. He held both my hands and looked me straight in the eyes as he reminded me once again that the Kingdom of Zerenity needed a leader, I was not to be taking any chances. I did my best to nod as if I agreed, but I wasn't sure that I did.

However, I knew that Zeid had been told to push the button if I didn't. Because even though I knew what Link told me was true, I wasn't sure I was ever going to be able to make that choice. Save myself at the expense of someone else? I didn't think I could do that.

Cahir was traveling with us. He and his wolf pack friends would help round people up if necessary. I hoped it wouldn't be, but I was happy that he would be walking with me for a while at least.

That left the Priscillas. Having recovered from their depression, which had turned out to be worry that they were infected, they were flitting around all of us as we made our plans. They wanted to go with me. At first Link and Niko said no, but when it became apparent that they would sneak off anyway, it was agreed that we could take them with us. I was delighted, and a little worried.

Although there was no evidence that the thought-worms had any use for fairy brains—so they probably weren't in danger that way—it was the violent crowds that had me worried. However, the Priscillas agreed to stay out of harm's way. They also argued that of all of us, they were most likely to see where the worms were coming from. Plus, they said they had a secret weapon that they would engage when we were ready.

Remembering the insects the Priscillas had recruited that had done the final job of eliminating the Shrieks, I thought that perhaps they had something like that up their sleeve that might save the day. I couldn't wait to see what they were planning.

The Ginete and the remaining Whistle Pigs were returning to their underground laboratory to take the bits of evidence that we would find and turn them into something useful for stopping Deadsweep.

Before Pita and Teddy left, they came over and each said good luck in their own way. Teddy swept me up in his massive arms and called me Warrior Princess. Pita patted me on the head and winked at me. They were the heroes in all of this. Without them, everything we did would mean nothing.

Finally, all the goodbyes were said. I grabbed my favorite walking stick as the ground opened up below us and the five of us dropped down into the underground transportation room. Even Cahir dropped with us. Zut, he was not happy. He started howling the minute we began to fall, and he didn't stop howling until we had returned to top side outside of the Castle. He shook himself and went off into the woods. He didn't come back to walk with me for a few minutes.

"Sorry," I projected to Cahir on his return.

"Necessary, but awful," Cahir projected back.

That pretty much summed up what we were doing. Necessary, but awful. I hoped that the awful wouldn't be too bad. But it was.

FORTY ONE

W e could hear Dalry long before we saw it. The noise was worse than anything I had ever heard. You'd think that the shrieking from the Shrieks would be at the top of the list and it was, but nothing sounded worse than what we could hear, because it was not a machine. It was human voices raised in anger and fright.

As soon as we heard it, we started running. The closer we got to it, the worse it got. It sounded like the three men we had first heard coming into Dalry, multiplied by one-hundred.

Every hair on my body stood up, and I could feel pulses of energy rushing through me. With my hand on Cahir's back, I could feel the same thing was happening to him.

Niko called a halt while we were still out of sight of Dalry. He tapped his ears, reminding us to keep our earplugs in. As if we would forget. I was continually scanning my body, looking for those ugly little worms. No worm was going to get on me. Ever. So disgusting in so many ways. Abbadon certainly knew how to push buttons. He could have made any kind of little machine to spread his Deadsweep infection. No, he chose a worm because of how most of us would feel about it—crawling into our brains. Yuck!

Cahir's ears perked up, and we all listened for what he heard. Footsteps were coming through the forest. Depending on how many people were coming we knew what to do. Zeid was carrying a supply of nets which he would shoot from what looked vaguely like a crossbow. Then Ruta would subdue them with a spray of the gas. Spraying gas in the open like that was tricky because we didn't want it blowing back on any of us. We chose Ruta to do the spraying because the gas didn't appear to affect him at all. Good thing worms didn't seem to like his kind either. If necessary, I wondered if we could get an army of Rutas.

Ruta looked at me as if I was crazy. "No army," he projected to me. "Got it," I responded.

We had all crouched behind trees so that whoever was coming wouldn't see us. Niko was ready with the nets and Ruta with the gas. Just as Niko was drawing his bow, I yelled, "Stop!"

I could see who had stepped out into the clearing. Hearing me yell, she screamed and pulled her children closer. It was Letha, the wife of the man that had been killed by his friends.

When I stepped out from behind the tree, she burst into tears. "Oh, zut, you scared me so much. We are trying to get further away from Dalry, and I didn't know what else to do but head towards the Castle and hope they let me in."

We all exchanged looks, and I invited her to sit on one of the always nearby rocks. Niko took out a container of water and offered it to them, along with one of the food bars we had with us. She took both but looked at them suspiciously.

"Are you worried they are infected?" I asked.

She nodded. "I decided to stay away from everyone after you all left. How did my husband get sick? I couldn't figure it out, so I decided not to do anything we normally did. We left the house, and we ate and drank only when necessary, praying each time that the food wasn't where that awful disease came from. But we are so tired and hungry."

They looked it. I wondered where Letha and her children had been sleeping, but whatever she did seemed to have protected her. After assuring her that the food and water were safe, they ate what we gave them. The children were barely moving. Their father had died, the town was in chaos, and they were tired, hungry, and terrified.

My hatred for Abbadon flared up, and a fireball flew out of my hand and landed by a pile of stones. This display of uncontrolled anger only served to scare the woman and her children so much they started crying again.

To me, Niko said, "Get a grip, Kara Beth. To them, you look infected. Besides, that kind of lack of control could get us all killed."

He was right. I scared the ziffer out of the people I wanted to help.

"I'm sorry," I whispered to the three of them huddled together, trying to protect themselves against me.

"I haven't quite got a handle on my skills yet, and the idea of what Abbadon is doing to my people made me angry."

They nodded as if they understood, but I could see that they were still afraid of me. Who could blame them? I was afraid of me.

Niko spoke to the woman and explained that we had a device that would determine if she or her children were infected. Could we use it?

Her nod was tentative. Of course, she wanted to know, and at the same time, she was afraid. What would happen if they were? Thankfully, none of them were, and when we told them, they all sagged in relief.

All of this was happening with the backdrop of screaming and yelling going on in the village, which was keeping us all on edge. But Letha had information we needed, and we weren't sure anyone else in the town would be free of the infection and could answer our questions.

Zeid knelt and put his arms around the little group. "You're safe now. We'll get you transportation back to the Castle where you will be taken care of. But before you go, could you answer a few questions for us? It would help us figure out how this is happening, and since you kept your family safe, what you did might be what we need to know."

She nodded and smiled. Probably the relief of not having the Deadsweep infection and knowing they would be safe, had just begun to dawn on her. She answered all our questions but didn't know as much as we hoped. Mostly she told us that right after we left, one by one people starting getting irritable, then grouchy, which rapidly progressed to violence.

She and her children had watched from a little hut that her husband had made as a playhouse for the children, not letting anyone know where they were. As the situation got worse, she stopped letting the children watch.

When we asked her what the three men had in common, at first she just stared at us. It was obvious. They were friends. They hung out together.

So Niko changed the question. What had the three of them done a few days before that no one else had done yet in the village?

Again, she said there was nothing. It was just a regular day. Of course, it was an ordinary day to her, but what did they do?

Niko asked her to walk through what her husband had done right before he started getting grouchy. We were hampered by the fact we didn't know how long it took for the thought-worms to take over. Should we be looking back a day, or two, or a week? We didn't know.

Then she said something interesting, and we realized we might be on the right track.

FORTY TWO

The moment we heard the noise coming from the village, the Priscillas had flown off. It would be nice to think that I have some control over what they do, but I doubted that anyone could control a fairy. I had to believe that they knew what they were doing and were safe. Maybe they went off to get their secret weapons.

In the meantime, Letha had remembered something. When we asked her to tell us what her husband and his two friends did a few days before they started getting sick, she told us about the traveler.

"A few days before the sickness, my husband had gone for a walk before dinner. He often did that. He loved watching how the seasons changed, and he said a nice walk through the countryside helped clear his head.

"He walked the roads rather than through the meadows and forest because he didn't like having to watch where he was stepping. He preferred daydreaming or meditation while he walked. He would return home at times, having stepped in a hole or have little burrs sticking to his pants that had to be picked off.

"A few days before he got sick, he met a man on the road who was selling some beautifully carved walking sticks. My husband loved the trades that happens between our villages. The walking sticks were lovely really, and I understood why he bought them. But we had enough walking sticks, so he gave them as gifts to his two friends."

Niko stepped in. "To be clear about this. Your husband bought two walking sticks, but then he gave them to his friends as gifts right away? He didn't leave them in the house for any length of time?"

"No, he just popped his head in, showed me the sticks and then took them over to his friends, and came back for dinner. The next morning he was grumpy, which was so unlike him."

"Did he say what the man looked like?" Zeid asked.

"Ordinary. Just a tradesman walking between villages. We get them all the time. We even have a few who live in our village and trade some of the things we make or grow with other villages. So meeting someone new wasn't unusual at all," Letha answered.

Turning pale, Letha asked what we were all thinking. "Was it something in the walking sticks? Did my husband bring this infection to our village?"

I put my arm around Letha. I could feel how thin she had become. She was shaking, and her children were huddled in her lap. "We don't know. No one knows. But even if it was in the walking sticks, your husband didn't bring the infection to Dalry. That man did. On purpose."

We hadn't proven that, of course, but it seemed pretty obvious. Somehow, this man brought the worms with him. Perhaps he didn't know what he was carrying. But if that was true, why wasn't he infected?

"Do you know where those sticks are now, Letha?" Niko asked.

"The last time I saw them, they were in the tavern. The men had them when they started fighting."

While we were talking, Niko must have summoned the Sound Bubble because I heard the sound of hundreds of notes playing in harmony coming towards us. I didn't think that I would ever tire of hearing that beautiful music. So opposite from what we could hear coming from Dalry.

I hugged Letha one last time, told her we would see her back at the Castle, and stepped away. I knew the three of them had never been in a Sound Bubble before. The joy on their faces was what I was sure I looked like the first time it descended over me and whisked me away.

We all waved to Letha and her two children and then turned to each other to discuss what to do next. Pris chose that moment to come flying out of the woods. She landed on my head, without even trying to slow down first, which meant her foot got tangled in my hair. As she righted herself, she pulled a few strands out.

I started to say "ouch," but then I saw her face. I wasn't sure I had ever seen Pris that upset before. La and Cil were right behind her, so I put my hands out for them to land on so that they wouldn't do the same thing on my head.

After taking a few deep breaths, Pris said, "You can't believe it. The town is almost gone. Buildings are burned down. People are lying in the street. Some of them look dead. There are even ..."

When Pris couldn't finish, La took over, "There are even children lying in the streets and fields. You have to stop it, but you can't go in there while all that is going on. People are ripping each other and themselves apart with their teeth."

"There is probably no one left there to save, but if they are, they are hiding somewhere, and you won't be able to find them with all those crazy people. They are like walking dead, no longer people," Cil said through her tears.

Niko took command. He told Link to broadcast across the Kingdom that under no circumstances was any villager to trade with a tradesperson of any kind until further notice. Niko told Link about the walking sticks. They decided to have any walking sticks acquired in the last few weeks carefully collected and burned immediately, or at the very least quarantined.

After he finished talking to Link, Niko turned to us as if looking for answers. We didn't have any, but I did have a question.

"Dalry appears to be the worst village so far, doesn't it?"

"What are you getting at, Kara?" Zeid asked.

"This is the closest village to the Castle. Do you think he came from there?"

FORTY THREE

"Why didn't the Mayor alert us as to what was happening in the village?" Zeid asked. "We gave him a communication device, but he never used it, did he?"

Niko shook his head. "No, he didn't."

The implications of what that could mean silenced us all for a beat. Either Mayor Tom had gone crazy right away, or he had been targeted and killed.

One other idea occurred to me, though. "Maybe he couldn't contact us for other reasons. Maybe he found a place to hide like Letha and her children did, and then he was afraid to make any noise. Or maybe someone took it from him, or he lost it."

Professor Link was ahead of me. "I think you could be right, Kara. I tracked the signal back to where the device is. You might find Mayor Tom there too. I don't want to break in and talk to him in case he is in hiding.

"And before you rush off to save him, it's possible someone else has it and is waiting for you."

That was a sobering thought. It meant some of the people in Dalry, knowing that we would return, were lying in wait for us. It was hard to believe that we had been there just a few days before and were warmly welcomed.

Things had changed quickly. Abbadon's plan to destroy all life would not take long at this rate.

After listening to what the Priscillas had seen, we decided we needed a different way to get into town. We had no intention of marching down the road to get there, but finding the perfect entry point was going to be tricky. We couldn't let ourselves be seen.

Even if we were not being purposely targeted, everyone who was alive was in danger from the people infected with the Deadsweep virus.

We still planned to rescue anyone who was not yet infected, starting with the Mayor. That was our priority. Once that was done, our next priority was to find and remove the walking sticks without contaminating ourselves. We didn't know for sure that it was the way Abbadon was transporting the worms, but we had to act as if it was.

We also had to assume that the worms were everywhere. Watching for them was going to be difficult while trying to avoid getting killed by a villager.

However, there was another possibility which eased our minds a little bit. It was a terrible thought, but one reason we might be safe from the worms was that they were all already in everyone's brain. We knew the thought-worms stayed inside the body even after the host died.

We knew that because before we left the Castle, the two men we had captured with Letha's husband had died, and until Pita froze the room, the worms did not come out.

We assumed that in the end, the worm's activity in the men's brains killed them. It didn't matter how it killed them because the result was horrible. The last few days had been a nightmare to watch, and we couldn't imagine what it felt like for the men.

The other reason we might be safer than it might appear we were was also morbid. If so many people were dead, how many were there left to come after us?

None of these scenarios made us feel any better. We might be safer because of the extent of the Deadsweep infection in Dalry, but that was a high price to pay.

It was Ruta who came up with the idea that none of us had thought about. However, given that Ruta knew how to travel by tree, it made sense that he was the one that suggested it. Traveling by tree was just what it sounded like, even though I didn't understand how it worked.

Ruta, Mr. Block-Of-Wood himself, traveled that way all the time when we weren't around. When he was with us, he chose to travel our slower way. On his own, Ruta would somehow merge with the tree and then pass through the roots, trunks, and limbs to get where he was going without being seen.

That's not what he was proposing for us to do, though. Good thing, because no one but Ruta could turn himself into some form of energy that traveled through the trees.

When he had first explained that process to me, it reminded me of the transporters in Star Trek, but instead of turning into energy that traveled through space, he moved through trees. When I first tried to explain the beam concept to Ruta, he looked at me as if I was an idiot.

"It was just a TV show," I tried to explain. It didn't help. TV shows didn't mean anything in Erda, and since no one could beam themselves places in real life, Ruta was not impressed. In Erda, people just left one place and arrived in another. Ruta had once tried to explain that one to me too, but what he said sounded like gibberish to me.

If all of us standing outside Dalry could do the leap-to-another-place thing, then we would have done it. However, none of us could—except for Zeid. But Zeid didn't know where he would leap to that would be safe, so after exploring Ruta's idea of using the trees, we decided it was the best plan that we had at the moment.

The forest we were in came to the edge of a meadow that extended all the way to Dalry. However, a grouping of maple trees meandered through the meadow all the way from the forest to the center of Dalry. With the trees' help, we would use what I used to call the squirrel highway.

In the Earth dimension, I loved watching the squirrels travel across the top of the trees, leaping from branch to branch, never touching the ground. We would do the same. Even though we were much bigger and nowhere near as nimble in a tree as the squirrels, the trees would help. The trees would make sure a branch was close enough and strong enough for us to move through the tree canopy into town without being seen.

That was the plan, anyway. We hoped that being in the trees would also make it easier for us to see places that people could be hiding without letting the other villagers know that we were there. The Priscillas planned to dart around without being seen and look for people who didn't appear to be infected with the virus.

If we found any, we would extract and test them. If they were free of Deadsweep, we would send them back to the Castle. If they were infected, we had another problem on our hands. How to round them up and where to keep them. The rounding up part was something that my bracelet was supposed to help with.

Given how dangerous the mission had become, I didn't think I could leave things to chance.

I asked Niko if I could practice with the bracelet now. I thought he would say yes. He didn't. He said it might attract attention, and

I was going to have to do it right the first time. Then he added that he trusted in me to get it done.

I held on to that thought as the first tree lowered its branches and we stepped up into another world.

FORTY FOUR

If we hadn't been on such a dangerous mission, the trip through the trees' overstory would have been glorious. I had heard of all the things found up in the canopy of trees, but had never seen it, and without the trees help, I wouldn't have been seeing it then, either. I vowed that when all this was over, I would spend more time up off the ground in the tree world.

We moved slowly to let the forest adjust to our presence and not give us away by any unusual bird or animal movements reacting to our being there. That meant we had time to stop and watch a bird feed its young, and examine a squirrel nest. We found plants that I thought only grew on the ground growing high up in the air.

Large amounts of dirt had accumulated in some of the larger trunk spreads, and plants of all kinds were growing in them. It was as if the birds had planted their own garden.

In other crooks of the branches, little ponds of water had gathered. We were waiting by one of those small ponds when I thought I saw something jump out of the water. I almost fell out of the tree when I realized it was a fish.

"How did a fish get up here?" I whispered to Ruta.

He didn't answer me, just pointed back to the pond where I saw there was more than one fish.

"What the ziffer?" I said, and then shut up as Niko gave me one of his looks.

In spite of his gazelle-like body, Niko looked perfectly at home in the tree. It was weird how he almost blended into the trunk of the trees. Sometimes I had to look twice to see the outline of his body.

Ruta also blended into the tree, but that was different. He was part tree. Niko was not. Or was he? Was he a shapeshifter or was he like a chameleon? And if he was one or the other, how come I didn't know that before?

Niko answered me in my mind. "You hardly know anything yet, Kara."

I would have made a face, but it was obviously so true I had nothing to say. My big comeback was, "So teach me!"

That was probably a mistake. Don't piss off a fairy was one thing. Making Niko a teeny tiny bit angry was a thousand times worse. At first I thought I was in deep trouble, but instead, he laughed. "Trying," he answered.

I realized in that one answer he had managed to put me down and encourage me at the same time. I guess that was one reason he was a master teacher.

"Thank you," was Niko's response to what I was thinking. That was the perfect response, so I had nothing else to say.

A few minutes later, the tree did what I could only call a shiver that ran all the way from its roots, up its trunk, and through its branches. We weren't in danger of falling off, but we all got the message. Be quiet.

Looking down through the tree's canopy, we saw two men. I didn't recognize them. They were trying to be stealthy, but were not doing a very good job of it.

Half the time, they were pushing and shoving at each other. One of the men growled at the other, which made me break out in goose bumps. I would not want to be on that guy's wrong side. Either one of them, actually.

"There's no one out here," one of the men said to the other.

"Zut," the other said. "Might as well keep going then. Heard the Castle has food."

"Yea. Lots of kinds of food and people!"

We understood what he meant. We all tuned in to Link back at the Castle as he said, "I heard that. We'll be on the watch for them, but they will probably kill each other before they get here. Still, glad you are all in the trees and not on the ground. Great idea, Ruta!"

Link was right. Those two would probably never make it to the Castle, but that didn't stop us from worrying. On the other hand, the fact that they were heading that way might mean that Deadsweep had done its worst in Dalry and the danger was mostly over. Dead people or uninfected people. Which would we find more of? I was pretty sure which one it would be.

As we moved through the trees' overstory, I tried to focus on the beauty and power of what we saw. This was nature at its finest. Birds, animals, plants, and even fish lived in the treetops, and Deadsweep had not reached any of them. So far at least.

I knew that once Abbadon felt he had the people of the Kingdom of Zerenity under control, either dead or dying, he would then focus on killing the rest of nature. He couldn't afford to let it remain, because he knew that sooner or later, if left alone, nature would find a way to destroy him.

That meant we didn't have any time to waste. We had to stop Deadsweep and then go after Abbadon himself.

Once we reached the maple trees in the meadow, our view changed. No longer could we see just the beauty of the canopy of the trees. Instead, we saw bodies lying in the field, and the destruction of the beautiful village of Dalry lay before us. It was so overwhelming that we all had to stop and take a breath. How could all of this happen in just a few days?

I heard a small rustle of leaves above and looked up to see the Priscillas. They looked like they were sliding down a beam of light.

I knew it was a trick of perception, but I took it as a symbol of the power of good—something we always needed to hold onto, especially in times like these.

"We found a small group of people hiding in a room in the schoolhouse," Pris said. "We think the Mayor may be part of the group because of what the note said."

"What note? How could you see them hiding in the schoolhouse when no one else did? How do you know it's not a trap?" asked Niko.

La looked at Niko like she was going to tweak one of his ears, but was polite instead.

"We know about traps, Mr. Niko," she humphed. "There was a tiny note taped to an outside window that told us he was in there. Besides, it's in the general location of the beacon that the Mayor was carrying."

At Niko's look, she added, "Yes, it could have been a trap, and someone else could have seen it, and that would have been a dangerous thing to do.

"But neither of those two things is true. No one but us could have seen it, being high up at the top of the ceiling, and it said, "Peach Blossom, Ten Teddy said you'd know what to do."

I knew what La meant. Only the Mayor knew about Teddy calling me funny names, so he mixed it up to tell us that ten people were in there somewhere.

"That's the good news," Cil said. "The bad news is there is a large group of infected near the schoolhouse. Some are guarding the doors. Most are hanging out in the classrooms.

"Well then, where would the Mayor be?"

"That's the part we don't know. You'll have to go in to find out."

"Past the infected," I said to myself.

"Yes, past the infected," the Priscillas answered.

FORTY FIVE

"This might be a good time to use the bracelet," Niko said.

Everyone's eyes swiveled to me. Not all of them were happy eyes. "I think I'll stay here," Ruta said.

When no one else said anything, I said, "Okay, everyone stays here. I would feel better about that, anyway."

I heard a low growl and saw Cahir at the base of the tree. "You too," I said to him. I knew that Cahir and his friends had surrounded the village, and their job was not to let anyone pass.

The two men we had seen in the woods had been trailed by one of the wolves until the two men had lain down under a tree and died. A rather peaceful death for someone infected with Deadsweep. I wondered if perhaps the trees had something to do with how easy it had been for them.

When a wave of peacefulness passed through me, I knew that was true. I hoped if something happened to me, it would be around a tree.

"Nothing is going to happen to you, Kara," Link said in my head. "You will do fine with the bracelet. Just take your time and don't get emotional about what you will see."

"What if I hurt someone?" I whined back at him.

"I'm coming with you," Zeid said. "Don't try to stop me. Instead, let me be your backup and guide if you need one."

We both looked at Niko, who nodded at the two of us, and Ruta rolled his eyes. The Priscillas clapped their hands together, looking as pleased as someone could be as they sent their friend off to try some magic that could go horribly wrong.

Niko was lying on a tree branch looking for all the world as if nothing was going on except an excursion into the woods.

I whispered to Zeid, "Don't Niko and Aki sometimes remind you of snakes?"

Zeid smiled back at me and didn't answer, but gave me a warning look when I started to respond. Zounds, Niko was right. The things I didn't know.

I tucked all those feelings of frustration, anger, and sorrow away where I could reach them when I needed them to light the flame inside of me. The fire that would help me with what I needed to do. Once that was done, I stepped into the next tree, with Zeid following me.

The noise from the village had quieted down. That was not good news. It meant more people had died. On the other hand, I also hoped that it meant there were fewer people around the schoolhouse. But once we could see the building, the opposite was true. Instead, it looked as if it had become the magnet for every infected person in town. Perhaps they could tell someone was inside that wasn't infected and they were stalking them? That was a scary thought.

Zeid and I dropped out of the tree as Zeid threw an invisibility shield around us. It was something I had learned to do for doors and buildings. I wasn't aware that it could be done for people or that Zeid knew how to do it either until the day before. The problem was Zeid couldn't hold it for long over people, and it took a lot of energy, so he would be vulnerable afterward if what I was going to do didn't work.

As we got closer to the group, I saw something that struck fear in my heart. The Mayor was part of the knot of men guarding the door. Zeid saw him too but motioned for me to do what needed to be done anyway. Maybe the Mayor was faking being infected. Or perhaps he was infected after he put up the note. Or maybe not. It could all be a trap. There was no way to find out except to go forward with the plan.

"Go, Kara," Zeid whispered. I looked up at him and then mentally closed my eyes.

Aki had drilled in me over and over again that closing your eyes was not a good idea. What would you miss as you shut the world away? Too dangerous.

Instead, I kept my eyes open, closed down the noise in my head, opened myself to the flow of energy coming from the earth and down from the sky. I felt the power of the millions of roots and beings that made up the planet, felt the spread of trees radiating life from their being, and then touched the picture jasper stone on my bracelet.

A small beam moved out, and I expanded it until it became a wall of energy. I pushed it towards the schoolhouse. The infected must have felt it coming, but there was nothing that they could do to stop it. I directed it until it circled the building, capturing everyone inside its radiance. Then sent one last blast of energy up from the ground, and everyone fell over. I hoped they weren't dead. I was going for stunned.

"It worked!" Zeid said.

He had dropped the invisibility cloak and looked drained. I could feel the residual power of the force field still vibrating inside of me, and without thinking, I touched his hand. Zeid jumped back, and I worried that I had hurt him. Instead, he smiled, rubbed his hand, and said, "Wow, that was weird, but now I feel great."

"Come on, we need to make sure they are all down, and find the others before these people wake up," I said, running toward the building. Inside of me, I was elated. So far, I hadn't hurt anyone. The bracelet worked. "Thanks, mom," I said to myself. It could have been the rush of energy or wishful thinking, but I thought I heard, "You're welcome."

There was no time to think about it. We reached the Mayor first. He was out. So was everyone around him. I sent a message to Niko to come with the nets. The plan was to wrap everyone before they woke up, and then drop them all down into the chambers that the Ginete and Whistle Pigs had prepared below us.

Within seconds, I saw Pita and his brothers coming through the schoolyard, prepared to help. As always, they were there when we needed them. I knew the Whistle Pigs were down below waiting for the bodies to be lowered to them.

Once the roundup began, our job was to find the uninfected, if there were any, and get them safely away to the Castle.

"Call out, we're here to rescue you," we all yelled, as we moved through the rooms in the schoolhouse, trying not to step on the inert bodies of the infected villagers, and watch for worms at the same time.

My blast from the bracelet was meant to affect only the infected villagers, so, if it worked properly the uninfected, would still be able to answer.

We were just about ready to give up, thinking that, yes, it had been a trap, when I heard a tiny voice say, "Is that you, Princess Kara Beth?"

I thought that I would never again complain about that name. "Yes!" I said.

We heard the squeak of a door coming from another room. When we got there, nine people, including five children, were waiting for us, looking frightened. I prayed they weren't infected.

"What happened to the Mayor?" I asked one of the children I had seen a few days before. "He went to get us food, and he never came back."

Forgetting all about infection, I gathered the child in my arms, and we cried together.

FORTY SIX

While the infected were being gathered and taken down to the rooms the Whistle Pigs had prepared for them, we were holed up with the drone in the schoolhouse. We tested the four adults and five children that had been hiding behind a wall in a coat closet. Thankfully, they were all free from the Deadsweep infection.

Amanda, the little girl who had cried with me, told us that they had gotten so hungry and thirsty the Mayor had risked going out to try to find food and water. He volunteered, even though he knew what could happen.

Somewhere along the way, a worm must have found him, and he had never returned. On the other hand, he had not led the infected to the people he was protecting. He knew that we were coming, but he didn't warn anyone. So, even while he was going crazy, he remained conscious of what he needed to do to save the people he had hidden.

That gave us hope that Mayor Tom, and maybe the other infected people, could be saved. However, based on what had happened with the other prisoners we knew we only had a few days before whatever the worms were doing to them, killed them.

We sent the nine infection-free people back to the Castle in a Sound Bubble and then dropped below to check on how the infected were doing and to find out if there had been any progress in discovering how to stop the worms and remove them. There had been thirty infected people at the schoolhouse. That combined with the nine we found meant that there were only forty-two people left in Dalry, counting Letha and her children. The death toll was staggering. If this were happening all over Zerenity, it would be devastating.

Ruta and Niko had found the walking sticks. One was in the tavern and one was lying outside the schoolhouse door. Niko wove a spell around each one of them, which encased them within something that looked like plastic, and then, without touching them, levitated them down with him into the lab where Pita and his brothers were working. Once there, they placed them behind a transparent barrier which allowed them to examine the walking sticks without physically touching them.

Somehow, the Whistle Pigs had prepared thirty rooms for the people from Dalry. I knew that they had to use some form of magic to get them built that fast. How did they know it was going to be thirty people?

We wished we could put the people together, but we already knew that wouldn't work. However, seeing those poor people isolated in their rooms was hard to take. Being isolated seemed only to make them crazier.

However, the Whistle Pigs said they were going to try all kinds of things to calm them down. We knew that the gas worked, but only for a time, and it certainly didn't make the thought-worms leave their hosts, which is what all of us wanted the most.

Once everyone was safe, we ate a quick meal, and then each of us went to our rooms for much-needed rest. Everyone except the Priscillas. Once again they were flying off on their own without telling me where they were going. But I had learned. Don't ask what they were doing. When they were ready, they would tell me.

A few hours later, our group met in the planning room to discuss what to do next. Pita was there with his report. Yes, the walking sticks had carried the thought-worms.

One of the sticks was empty of worms, but the one by the schoolhouse still had a few thought-worms left in it.

That was a piece of good news. First, that no one in our group had picked it up and became infected, and second, that the sticks still had worms they could study that hadn't been activated yet.

"On the other hand, since the walking stick with the worms was the one found by the schoolhouse, it is probably how Mayor Tom became infected. He might have seen it there, picked it up to defend himself and in the process became infected," Pita said.

Niko stood. "Here's what we know now. We know the walking sticks are carrying the worms, and that at least one tradesman is bringing them to the villages."

"Why isn't that tradesman infected?" I broke in.

"That's a good question," Niko said. "But a question that we might not be able to answer until we capture him, or them, if there is more than one. And, Kara Beth, you mentioned something we need to think about. Did he come from the Castle? Is it someone we know?

"The dragons have reported that the villages further away from the Castle are less infected. That does imply that it is just one person moving outward from the Castle. Or he could be targeting the communities where we have been, or where our families live.

"Also, no one could walk this quickly. So if it is just one person, he's using another mode of transportation to get to each village."

"Like Leif, Sarah, and Zeid can do?" I asked.

"Possibly something like that," Niko responded. "Which makes him someone who is skilled at using magic."

"Which makes him even more dangerous," Zeid said.

"Why would someone support Abbadon like that?" I asked. "What would anyone else get out of destroying all life? What could Abbadon have promised him to make him be an instrument of destruction this way?"

"Of all the people here, Kara, you'd think you would understand it best," Niko said. "You've been to the Earth dimension where power and greed take over someone's thinking, and the result is the destruction of life. Perhaps no thought-worms are doing this in the Earth Realm, but something destroys the goodness inside of those people bit by bit.

After that, there is no longer any rational thought or feelings involved. It's just evil. The person they were before is gone. Walking dead, skinwalkers, whatever you want to call them. Here in Erda, we have Abbadon reproducing this destruction in an obvious way. Quite symbolic, really."

I knew what Niko was talking about. For all the goodness found in most people, in the Earth dimension, there were those who were so out of touch with their humanity that they were systematically destroying life. Not as directly as what was happening in Erda, but it was the same thing.

In a way, this was easier, at least for the moment. We knew who had started it.

I knew who was going to end it, too. We would stop it. We had to, or everything would die. There was no way I was going to let that happen.

FORTY SEVEN

"What is the news for Eiddwen and Kinver?" I asked. I found it suspicious that we hadn't had any reports from either team who had gone to those towns. When Niko hesitated, I knew that I was right, and I steeled myself for upsetting news.

"We have no news," Niko finally said.

I looked at Ruta and Zeid and knew that they were already aware of that fact.

"And you didn't tell me, why?" I fumed. "Obviously, I am the only one who doesn't know."

Professor Link broke in. "It was my choice, Kara. We needed you to stay focused on dealing with Dalry and using your bracelet to access that power to stun, but not kill. If you would have been a little upset, I wasn't sure if you might have miscalculated."

As much as I didn't want to admit it, I could see that Link had a point. I had struggled to release just the right amount of power. But that didn't excuse the delay in telling me. We had been back for hours.

"Okay, I concede that it might have been a good idea to withhold the information from me then, but why the wait?"

Niko was the one who answered. "That was my choice. You would have wanted to rush off without eating and resting, both of which you will need to be effective. Besides, there were things we could do from here, and the Ginete and I did that while you three rested."

There was no point in continuing to argue, so I just allowed myself a tiny pout and a bigger flame of anger that I stored away before I asked the obvious question.

"What did you find out, and when are we leaving?" I asked.

Niko smirked. "I rest my case. You want to rush off?"

"No, I don't. I want to know first, and then I want to rush off."

"Which place are you going to first?" Niko asked.

"You mean both teams are not reporting in?" I asked, realizing that was what Niko had said in the first place, but it hadn't registered.

"There could be multiple reasons why they are not connecting to Link's channel. They could have turned it off on purpose. Maybe they discovered something about our communication that meant it was safer not to be connected," Niko answered.

"Or maybe someone turned it off for them," I responded sarcastically. Sarcastic was a better choice for me at the moment, because otherwise my voice would have trembled and I might have broken down into a sobbing ball of uselessness. The idea that Suzanne and Aki or the brothers and Beru were in danger and we weren't there to help threatened to be paralyzing. Which one would we choose to go to first?

"They might have," Niko said. "But all of them are capable of taking care of themselves, so we are going with that they are staying quiet for a reason."

"So, still my question is, which one are we going to first?" I asked, a little less snarky.

"Neither yet. We are waiting for a report from Teddy and Pita. We will need more information before we go rushing in," Niko said.

"How long are we going to wait, though?" I asked, thinking that I was leaving no matter what they said.

"Not long, Pink Ears. We have a few things that we think will help."

We left right after Teddy showed up at the meeting calling me Pink Ears. The Priscillas returned from wherever they had been and practically fell into my pocket and promptly went to sleep. I was just happy to have them back with me before we left.

But we weren't going to either town. We were going back to the Castle. The best part of that decision was that we got to ride in the Sound Bubble to get there. Despite the terror of what was going on, I couldn't help but feel a surge of joy as the bubble descended, rose, and zoomed us back to see Ariel and Earl.

That's the other funny thing about the bubble. If you looked at the Sound Bubble, you would think that it would float slowly to wherever it was going, like a hot air balloon. But it didn't. It covered the distance between Dalry and the Castle in just a few minutes, as it always did.

I know I am dense, but I had never stopped to think about how that was happening.

There was no visible sign of a motor or a steering mechanism. The Sound Bubble would show up, and take us where we were going. No one was driving it. I wasn't even sure who it was that was calling it to pick people up. This unawareness was another example of what Niko had said. I didn't know much, and that probably made me more dangerous than it made me helpful.

"Not really," Zeid said, squeezing my hand. "But not knowing can be very dangerous, just like rushing off is not ever wise." Niko turned his face from us, so I knew he wasn't ready to interfere with this assessment, even though I knew he agreed with it.

Although I loved the bubble, Ruta hated it. He always had to do his best not to look as if he wasn't going to throw up. It was funny how Ruta could be high up in a tree without a thought, but in the Sound Bubble, all his fear of heights showed up.

I tried to hold his hand, but he rebuffed me. I didn't take it personally. I have called Ruta Mr. Grouch Head more times than I could count, but Ruta was our healer, our rock, the one who hid his deep compassion by doing his job. Showing weakness did not fit into Ruta's personality. I could understand that, and I admired it.

I wished I was less volatile, less displaying of all my emotions out in the open for everyone to see.

Since it only took a few minutes to get back to the Castle, I didn't have a chance to find out how the bubbles worked. But I did have a thought that perhaps they were like the portals. Somehow, they manipulated time.

Niko glanced over at me and touched his nose. Huh, I might be onto something, I thought. That meant I had a question that might help with the thought-worms, and I almost started to ask it. But then Niko shook his head, and in my head, I heard him say, "Not now." I nodded. I understood. Later.

Instead, we all looked down at the glass ceiling of the atrium as it opened and we lowered into the garden where Leif and Sarah were waiting for us. Like the Sound Bubble, it was hard not to be happy to see the two of them, even though I knew that what they had to tell us might be horrible.

Still, they smiled and waved, and we all waved back, even Ruta.

FORTY EIGHT

One thing that I had learned from Leif and Sarah—both in the Earth Realm where they had been "ordinary people" with extraordinary gifts, and now in Erda where one was a Wizard and the other an Oracle—was that some things are more important than others.

And waiting for an answer was the most important thing we could do at that moment. It didn't mean that I liked it. But I knew that they were right. Sometimes that answer was immediate, other times it took time. But without that answer that came from the still small voice within, an Earth term that Sarah still used in Erda, there was a chance we would be doing the wrong thing.

That didn't mean we wouldn't do something. Pausing to listen was good, stalling was something else, and I often didn't know the difference. Or at least that's what I'd been told before, and the fact that I was feeling the impatience eating at me, told me I hadn't yet learned to listen.

"Oh, I wouldn't say that," Sarah said, as she hugged me after I stepped out of the bubble. "You often listen; it's just that your listening usually takes place in dreams."

"Or daydreams," I added.

Sarah nodded in agreement and said, "So don't discount those flashes of insight, Kara Beth. Not everyone listens in the same way. And internal instruction doesn't always arrive when we are still.

"For some people, action is the door that opens the way for wise instruction. The trick is being able to discern which is which."

Standing in the garden with Sarah was so lovely I almost forgot why we were there. But the arrival of Earl and Ariel was enough to remind me. I couldn't decide if the fact that they were there too made me more afraid or less afraid.

Earl laughed, and his laughter rolled through all of us like a wave of thunder and I felt better immediately. I almost set off a bolt of lightning just to participate in the idea of a storm with thunder, but that seemed a touch too playful, and perhaps a bit dangerous.

Zeid, knowing how tempted I was to be a little mischievous, shook his head at me and I rolled the energy back. Maybe after this was over, Earl and I could play? I wondered what that would be like.

"Looking forward to it, little one," Earl pushed into my thinking. Earl made the phrase "little one" sound so endearing that tears sprung to my eyes in response.

Leif raised his staff and used it to point at the table. "We'll eat, you'll sleep, and in the morning we will put Teddy's plan into action."

"Not tonight?" I blurted out. Of course, I knew it was the wise thing to do. After all, this had been a long day. It was only that morning that we had headed into Dalry, and the sun was setting as the bubble had lowered itself into the atrium.

Perhaps Sarah's mention of dreaming was a reminder that some pieces of information would come to me, and maybe others, while we slept. But the worry that something might be wrong with my friends was eating at me so much I was anxious to go.

"It won't work at night anyway," Niko said, "And you know it."

The Priscillas chose that time to wake up and stretch. La must have forgotten that she was in my pocket because, as she stretched with her eyes closed, she started to fall out. I caught her, and everyone laughed, except La, who looked embarrassed.

Pris, being the protective older sister, put her arm around La, hugged her and then the three of them flew off to the table for their fairy food that was always there.

When no one moved to join them, the Priscillas circled back and started pulling everyone's hair, except Ruta, who didn't have any hair to pull. Instead, they knocked on his head until he began to move forward.

Once our feet started moving towards the table and I could see and smell the feast that had been laid before us, I realized how hungry I was. So I led the way, almost running the last few steps.

A metal toadstool was by my side within seconds with extra food, and I was so happy to see it, I patted it on the shoulder, or what passed as a shoulder.

I knew they were machines, but that didn't mean it didn't have feelings and I was sure that this was the one that almost always waited on me. I had named it George, and when I said, "Thank you, George," I swear it smiled at me. Or at least sent smile vibes.

I wasn't the only one that was hungry. No one spoke as we all dived in. When the first round of hunger was satisfied, I asked about the people we had sent back in the Sound Bubble.

"They are all resting comfortably," Sarah said. "Amanda asked me to give this to you."

Sarah reached into her pocket and pulled out a note and handed it to me. It was simple, and in a child's handwriting, but it broke my heart.

It said, "Thank you for coming for us, Princess Kara Beth. The Mayor said you would. I hope you can save him, too." It was signed by Amanda and she had drawn hearts all over the page.

I hoped we could save him, too. It was why I was so anxious to go. I knew that we only had a few days at the most to get the thought-worms out of the infected people. But first, we had to stop the infection from spreading. The Ginete and the Whistle Pigs had figured out how to stop the Shrieks and Shatterskin so their plan might work for Deadsweep too.

The problem was, no matter how good their plan was, we were the ones that had to execute it.

"And that's why you need to sleep first," Sarah said, getting up from the table.

As I walked back to my room, I missed Beru so much it was painful. She always walked with me and then said goodnight at the door. Zeid wanted to walk with me, but I had shrugged him off.

It was amazing that he still liked me. I didn't mean to be cruel, but sometimes the need to do what had to be done was the only thing driving me. Zeid and I would have to wait. I had to trust that he would understand because I wasn't so sure that I did.

FORTY NINE

I was so tired I thought I would fall asleep right away, but instead, in my mind, I ran over and over again what Pita and Teddy had planned for us to do. It seemed simple enough. They had tested it on a small scale so they didn't see why it wouldn't work on a large one. But there it was again. It was easy to test something in a relatively closed environment, but what about out in the real world?

Although I thought I hadn't slept at all, Pris, sitting on my face prying my eyelid open, told me that I had. I would have said something harsh to Pris, but that would have made her even more excited about doing it again.

The only way to get Pris to stop doing something I didn't like was to pretend that I did. As hard as that was, it was easier than getting Pris to do something I wanted her to do. No amount of begging or asking or demanding would ever get Pris to do something unless she chose it herself.

There were times I thought she wasn't really like that. Instead, she was showing me what stubborn looked like. Other times, I wasn't so sure. Maybe Pris was the poster child for the phrase, "don't tell me what to do." Anyway, this time I pretended that I loved her sitting on my face playing with my eye, even though my first response was to shove her off with one hand and strangle her with the other.

At least I had her confused, because when I smiled at her and said "good morning," she looked at me, trying to figure out if I was playing her. I kept my mind closed so she wouldn't hear me thinking, "Gotcha!"

I had showered the night before, and clean clothes were waiting on my bed. At least this time, I knew I had undressed myself. In the past, I hadn't been so sure. I still hadn't gotten to know the person, or people, in the Castle who took care of all these background things for me, like clean clothes and unlimited food. I hoped they would forgive me for not thanking them personally because, for now, all my attention was on Abbadon. Someday it wouldn't be.

Teddy had told us that the Priscillas had a solution for cleaning up all the thought-worms, but we had to disable the worms first. That was what we were up to today. We were going to Kinver to find the brothers and Beru and try out the latest gadget from the Ginete and Whistle Pigs scientific team. We had to trust that Aki and Suzanne were handling whatever was going on in Eiddwen.

However, the fact that they hadn't called for the Sound Bubble to bring my father back to the Castle was worrisome. But, I couldn't go there in my thinking at the moment. Maybe bringing him back to the Castle wasn't needed because there were no thought-worms in Eiddwen. That's what I told myself anyway.

Even though the Kingdom was in trouble, I knew that some of the Ginete and Whistle Pigs were in what we called in the Earth Realm, "hog heaven."

Never before had they been called upon to invent so many new things, or find answers to what seemed to be unanswerable questions. Abbadon had done them a favor. He had awakened a skill in them that they hadn't had a chance to use before.

When this was all over, I wondered what they would do with their awakened curiosity and ability to provide solutions to problems. I knew it couldn't be stuffed back into the bottle. We would have to find a beneficial reason for them to continue to invent cool tools.

Their latest invention was designed to disrupt the signals directing the thought-worms. After experimenting with the worms that had not yet entered a host body, they found a way to stop them from moving. That meant they wouldn't be crawling into anyone's ears. That was the good news. The bad news is that it didn't remove the worms from the people's heads. Once in there, something else was running the worms.

Once again, we were working with Earl and Ariel. Earl, or Coro as the commander of the storms, didn't need salt water this time, just walls of water. Because wireless signals don't pass through water easily, he and Ariel would build a wall of water around the town of Kinver.

The idea was that Abbadon wouldn't be able to direct any worms inside the wall of water. We would only have to deal with the programming already running in the thought-worms themselves. Inside the wall of water, we would stop the remaining worms with the devices that Teddy had brought us.

They were tiny hand-held transmitters designed to disable the signals running the machines inside the worms. I would be ramping up the voltage using my famous, fabulous, ability to produce lightning. I said it that way to myself to give myself courage. If I couldn't generate enough electrical charge, the transmitters might not be strong enough to disable the signals inside those disgusting worms. So there was no choice but to make it happen.

Once we stopped the thought-worms, I was supposed to use the power of the bracelet to stun the infected. Then they would be netted and dropped below into the holding rooms prepared for them. It was a repeat operation of what we had done at the schoolhouse, only this time we were ready to deal with the worms themselves.

It doesn't sound hard at all, I said to myself. But the fact that I had to generate two sources of energy worried me.

There would be one more step that the Priscillas had been working on that would get rid of all the stunned thought-worms for good. I had heard rumors that it was much like the insects that ate the melted green blobs that had been the Shrieks. But I had no idea what they were planning to use. I just hoped it didn't involve me doing any more energy releasing. In spite of assurances from the rest of the team that they would be helping, I was worried out of my mind that I wouldn't have enough power, energy, magic, or whatever it was to pull off the plan.

That left Leif and Sarah staying at the Castle working on removing the worms from the infected without killing the host. Niko had confided in me that they were playing with the idea of time, along the same lines as the Sound Bubbles and the portals.

There was nothing I could do to help them. I had to concentrate on what we were going to do. Trying to make it simple for myself, I thought that all we had to do was stop the thought-worms, disable the infected, save the town, and then the Kingdom. *Oh, yeah. Easy.*

FIFTY

After Pris pried my eyes open, she told me that everyone was meeting in the atrium for food, and then we were leaving. One thing no one had told me yet was how we were getting to Kinver. I assumed either by Sound Bubble or dragons.

It was just getting light outside by the time we had eaten. I had to force myself to eat. I knew that without food, my energy level would only last so long, magic or no magic. Teddy made sure our transmitters were in order. Link checked my bracelet, which didn't really need any checking. I think he just wanted to make sure I knew he would be watching over us.

Once everyone settled in, Link asked, "Are you ready?" I nodded, but I still didn't hear a Sound Bubble or see any dragons. Finally, I asked, "Okay, I give up. How are we getting there?"

"Well," Zeid said, coming up beside me and holding my hand. "Like …"

That's all I heard before I felt for a split second that I was coming apart and then put back together again. But not in the atrium. Somewhere else. But I knew where I was. We were on the road that overlooked Kinver.

"What the ziffer? Zut, and confound it. Couldn't someone have told me that was going to happen? Phew. What was that?" I said, as I bent over at the waist, trying not to faint.

"Pretty fun, huh?" Zeid said.

"No. Not so much," I answered, wishing I could slap the smile off of everyone's faces. On the other hand, Zeid, Niko, and Ruta looked so pleased with themselves I ended up smiling at them. "Okay, it was a little fun. But how did you do that?"

Niko answered, "It's Zeid's thing. We just went along with it. Since he brought all of us with him this time, we're going to give him a minute to recharge. But this was the fastest way and the least obvious."

All I could think of was how much I wanted to learn how to do that myself. While we waited for Zeid to recover, I looked around thinking about the last time I was on this road. I had just left Eiddwen and was coming to visit the people of Kinver. At that time, I would never have guessed that I would return this way, or for this reason.

After a few minutes, Zeid said, "Okay, I'm ready," and we started walking towards the town. I thought that it would've been better not to be so out in the open, but Link had worried about us walking through the brush in case the thought-worms were waiting there. And traveling the tops of trees wasn't an option this time. Meadows surrounded Kinver, not trees.

I knew that Cahir and his wolf pack had run across the country the day before to be here with us, and once again, they would watch the perimeter of the village. Their job was to keep all the villagers inside, infected or not infected. Up above us, I could see dragons circling, but without Suzanne, I didn't know how to talk to them.

The one problem with our disrupting plan was that we might also disrupt our signals between Link and our team. But it was something we were going to have to put up with. Once we turned off the disruption, we would be connected again.

As we got closer to town, we could see that something was wrong. But it was not what we expected. Unlike Dalry, which had been completely destroyed, Kinver looked perfectly normal. All the buildings were there, and the gardens were well tended. Except there weren't any people around—not one. The closer we got, the more Kinver looked like a ghost town.

Our plan had been designed to stop worms, and disable the infected, but what if that wasn't what was happening here? What were we going to do? Where was Beru? What about John, James, Thomas, and Pete? Or Liza and her mother? Where were the people of Kinver?

There was nothing. It was even more frightening than what we found in Dalry. At least there we knew what was going on. In Kinver, we were clueless. No worms. No people. Nothing.

Behind us, Coro and Ariel waited with the walls of water, which were useless until we found the worms. What had Abbadon done here? Had Deadsweep already killed everyone? And if so, where were they?

It was Ruta who saw the problem first. He had been looking towards the forest that circled Kinver, while we were focused on the town.

"Stop," he said, and pointed towards the trees in the distance.

We all turned to look and saw nothing other than trees. But something didn't seem right.

"Are those trees moving?" I asked.

"Yes," Ruta answered. "But those aren't trees."

"Zut!" Niko screamed. I had never heard Niko scream before, but I knew why he had. What looked like trees were moving faster, towards us, closing a circle around us. We were trapped.

"Can you get us out of here, Zeid?" Niko whispered.

At the same time, I called out to Link. "Do you see what is happening?"

There was no answer. Nobody could hear us. Whatever had kept Beru from staying in contact was preventing us from contacting Link.

"Zeid," Niko whispered again.

"I can't," Zeid said through clenched teeth. "I have no power at all."

I didn't either. It was as if a switch had turned off everything magical or powerful thing about me. I had nothing.

We watched helplessly as the moving, twitching things came closer, encircling us. To our horror, what had looked like trees from a distance were writhing worms. What was moving them, I didn't know. All I could see was the millions of worms heading our way. All for us. It took just one to make us crazy. Maybe these worms would do more than that.

I had one thought. We had to get help. I peeled the button that Link had given me off my skin, and before anyone could object, I stuck in on Zeid and pushed it. Within a split second, Zeid had disappeared. I hoped it was true that it would take him directly to Link. It was our only chance.

"Good thinking, Kara Beth," Niko said. "But you should have gone."

I shook my head. If we died that day, Zeid would make an excellent king, and I would have saved at least one person that I loved. That would have to be good enough for me.

The three of us stood back to back, waiting for the worms. I hoped it would be over quickly, but I had a feeling that Abbadon didn't plan it that way.

We held hands, and I prayed.

FIFTY ONE

All sorts of thoughts flashed through my head as that wriggling tree of worms came closer. Maybe it was true that before you die, you see your whole life flash before you. Because in those few minutes as I watched those ugly things inch their way towards us, I saw myself as the child called Hannah that I had been back in the Earth Realm.

I watched myself playing with Ben, my little brother. I saw myself hug my dad as he read to me out on the back deck. My mom was in the kitchen making cookies for us. It was all so normal. No wriggling, smelly, disgusting worms were working their way across our yard to do whatever horrible thing they were going to do to us.

I forced myself back to the present. Those times were over. It was here and now that I had to deal with. I remembered Aki telling me to keep my eyes open. I didn't want to. If I lived through this, I knew that picture would forever be burned into my brain. My hatred for a man, if Abbadon could be called a man, was fueling that familiar fire inside of me. I waited for it to surge up through the ground and out through my hands, thinking I could at least blast one tree and we could run past it to safety. But nothing happened.

"We seem to be in a force field of some kind," Niko said.

"Then how come I can smell those things?" I asked through clenched teeth.

"I think Abbadon is projecting that so that we will feel even more afraid," Ruta said.

By then, the worm trees were less than five feet away. If I would have stretched out my arm, I might have even touched one that was reaching towards us, but I'm not that crazy. I still had hope that Zeid had returned to the Castle and Link would be sending reinforcements. "You better hurry," I said to Zeid, and then in case he was listening, I added. "Since I haven't told you this, let me tell you now before it's too late: I love you."

Two things happened. First, a wall of water fell on us. So much water that if I had opened my mouth, I might have drowned. Then, as we were sputtering and trying to breathe through water, I felt something grab me by the shoulders and pull me straight up into the air.

Too frightened to scream, I watched as the wall of water continued to fall over the worm trees. As we moved sideways through the air, dangling from what I could see now were dragon claws, I watched what happened on the ground. The tree of worms stopped moving and then began to fall over until a huge pile of worms lay on the ground. Or at least that was what it looked like because by then we were so high up it was hard to see what was happening.

As grateful as I was to not be in the middle of those worms, flying through the air in the clutches of dragons was not a picnic, either. Their claws were digging into my shoulders, and I started to shake from the cold, and probably the shock of what had almost happened.

Watching Ruta and Niko fly through the air almost made it worth it, though. Ruta had his hands over his eyes. Poor Ruta. On the other hand, Niko was acting like he was a bird. His arms extended, his coat flapping in the breeze, a big smile on his face. Who knew Niko had a secret wish to fly?

Even though it seemed an eternity, it was probably only a few minutes until the dragons reached the forest. They carefully lowered each of us into a waiting tree which had kindly opened its massive trunk to receive us. Once we were settled, the dragons released us, and the tree closed again. Within minutes I felt warm and comfortable as the tree sent waves of heat to us. I felt as if I could stay there forever. I sent a prayer of thanks to the dragons hoping they could hear me, and leaned into the tree and kissed it. The tree shivered, and I giggled. It was a release of tension and an overflowing sense of gratitude for the community of beings who had protected us.

Still, we weren't out of danger. Our communication with Professor Link was still down, and I still didn't have any connection to my magic.

"Guess Zeid made it back to the Castle," I said, to break the silence that threatened to pull us down into despair. "He must have been able to communicate with Coro and the dragons, but they still don't seem to be able to talk to us."

Ruta hummed at me. It reminded me of the first time I had heard Ruta talk in what I thought might have been his native language. I hadn't understood a word as he and Beru had talked together. So when he started humming I realized that perhaps he wasn't humming to me, maybe he was talking to someone else. And then it occurred to me. The tree. He was talking to the tree.

Niko and I looked at each other, and back to Ruta who seemed to be getting more excited. Knowing Ruta as someone who didn't display any emotions, I wasn't sure if he was getting excited happy or excited scared.

I was both. I was excited happy and I was scared. I was warm and dry and protected in the tree, but where was everyone else?

We were missing a whole village. People I knew and had come to love were gone. People that we all had come to love. My heart broke a little for Ruta because I realized he was missing his best friend, Beru. They were inseparable, and she was gone too.

Ruta stopped humming and turned to Niko and me and said, "I know where the town is."

The fact that Ruta was not smiling was terrifying. What did he know that made him tremble? Were we going to be able to do anything about it, or were they gone forever?

I almost didn't want to know, because once I did, it might be something final with no hope left.

FIFTY TWO

After saying he knew where the townspeople had gone, Ruta stopped talking. Niko and I waited. And waited.

"Aren't you going to tell us?" I finally asked. My head didn't want to know, but my heart did.

"No," Ruta said, and then leaned back onto the tree trunk and closed his eyes.

I looked at Niko who shrugged and leaned back onto the tree trunk that was holding him up and closed his eyes, too.

"Are you both crazy?" I hissed. "What good is this?"

Neither one moved. If anything, the two of them snuggled closer into the tree trunk. I'm dense, I know. It's crazy how long it took me to get the message. Neither Niko nor Ruta ever did anything by chance. They both had laid their lives on the line over and over again to save the Kingdom from Abbadon. Whatever they were doing at that moment was not because they were apathetic. They were telling me something.

I wiggled around to get more comfortable and leaned back against my tree trunk, and closed my eyes. Nothing. In fact, so much nothing, I fell asleep. Or I fell somewhere because I knew I was still in the tree, and at the same time, I was standing in the middle of Kinver. But I wasn't alone. It was as if I had pressed my star, or shifted my focus to see the 4D world because not only could I see the homes and gardens, but the rainbow of colors that made up everything from the rocks in the road, to the earth in the garden.

Everything was intertwined. This was a view that I had seen before, but never quite like this, and never because I fell asleep in a tree.

Someone called out, "Hannah," and I turned to see James standing with his daughter, Liza. James looked as if he was frozen, his eyes wide open but seeing nothing. It was Liza who had called out. Liza, who has the gift of seeing 4D whenever she wants to. Liza smiled with her eyes but didn't move. She was frozen too, which meant she couldn't move her mouth to talk. Instead, she sent me words. They floated out of her and landed on my hand.

"We are here. Frozen and invisible to regular sight."

I turned around and around, and everywhere I looked people were frozen within what looked like a web of black threads. Abbadon. I knew it was him. Only Abbadon would be this cruel. Freeze a whole town. Locked between life and death, knowing neither, and no way out. Or was there?

Words from Liza drifted over to me again, but my vision was fading, so I only caught one word until the whole scene was gone. The word I heard was "portal."

All three of us opened our eyes at the same time, and Niko and Ruta looked at me expectantly.

"You're right, Ruta. We do know where the town is. Do you have any ideas on how to rescue them?"

Ruta shook his head. "Not a clue. Do you?"

I shook my head no. We needed help figuring it out, which meant we needed to get back to the Castle. At that moment I heard the most beautiful sound in the world as the hundreds of notes hummed in harmony getting louder and louder until it was directly over us. I looked up and saw Zeid. Tears poured down my face. He made it, and he had come for us.

We would find a way. We had to.

What I didn't tell Ruta was that right before the vision faded I had seen Beru, hanging in the air, tangled in the black threads. Beru looked like a flower trapped in a weed. That weed could be destroyed. I was positive. It had something to do with portals.

There was chaos back at the Castle. It seemed as if everyone who had been brought to the Castle for protection was running through the atrium going somewhere. It was so crazy, the bubble had to land inside the practice yard so we wouldn't get trampled.

"What the ziffer is going on," I asked Leif as soon as the bubble landed. The short ride over, I had enfolded myself in Zeid's arms which I thought was a place I wanted to stay. But the chaos below and the bubble landing had interrupted that.

Zeid laughed, "Well, I think they are happy."

"Happy? Why?" I asked and then realized that the people in the Castle didn't know about the frozen people caught within the black web. "Did something happen with the thought-worms?"

"Yep!" Pita said, coming up and shaking all our hands as if we had done something. "Come see," he said, stepping on one of the circles outlined in blue that had appeared in the yard. We dropped down into the transportation room filled with people. I recognized some of them from the village of Dalry. They were taking turns being transported up into the Castle. No wonder people were happy.

"You got the worms out! How?"

Instead of answering, Pita led us back to their lab where Teddy was standing, looking as pleased as I had ever seen him.

"Turtle Toes," he yelled, coming over to hug me. Who could stay unhappy after being called Turtle Toes by a giant Whistle Pig? Not me. For a moment, I forgot everything and let myself feel the joy that was vibrating throughout the tunnels.

"Once we figured it out, it was easy. Although there were a few moments that we thought it didn't work and that we were killing them because at first everyone had what looked like a seizure. But then the worms fell out of their ears. We were afraid that the thought-worms had permanently damaged their brains, but Leif did something, and everyone stood up and was fine. Weak, but fine."

When I turned to Leif to ask him what he did, he shook his head, and I understood that he wasn't going to tell us yet what he had done. We had a bigger problem to solve right now. The worms were out of the infected, but Abbadon was controlling the village of Kinver, and I suspected, Eiddwen too which is why we hadn't heard from Aki and Suzanne. The thought-worms were still out there, and people were frozen in time and space. We could celebrate this victory later.

Leif thanked Pita and Teddy and directed the four of us back up to the surface and into a quiet room where Earl, Ariel, and Sarah were waiting. I told them the story of what I had seen and what Liza had tried to say to me.

"Portal? What did she mean by that?" Zeid asked.

"That is what we are going to find out," Leif answered.

I hoped that Abbadon felt the rumble of our determination. I prayed that it scared the ziffer out of him. I wanted him to be terrified. I was tired of being terrified of him. We would figure it out, and then I was going after him, even if I had to go after him on my own.

There have been times when I haven't wanted everyone in my head, but this was not one of them. In unison, they had all answered, "You won't be on your own."

Yes, we were coming after him. But first, we had a few towns to unfreeze, and a million worms to destroy.

FIFTY THREE

Leif had asked us all to meet him in the planning room after we got cleaned up. The three of us definitely did not smell good. That worm smell was all over us. I took the fact that Zeid hugged me anyway to mean either he had lost his ability to smell things, or maybe he really loved me.

"Of course, I do, Kara," Zeid said stopping in the middle of a hallway. He had stayed by my side since I had stepped into the bubble.

"Have you ever doubted it?"

It was time to tell him the truth. "I can't remember how we came to be a couple, Zeid. Did we choose each other or did someone choose for us?"

"Does it matter?"

"Yes. It does to me," I answered.

"Would it mean that I loved you less if someone chose for us, Kara? What if they knew who we were to each other—who we always were to each other—and made sure that we found each other? Made sure that we didn't make a mistake and forget our destinies together?"

I had to think about that. Did it matter? Then I realized I had missed the essential parts of what Zeid had said.

"We have a destiny together?" Slapping my forehead, I added, "I'm incredibly dense aren't I? It's what we have been doing since I came through the portal, isn't it?"

Zeid lowered his forehead to mine and whispered, "And Kara, destiny or not, chosen for us, or by us, you must feel that I have always loved you.

"And you can't keep it a secret anymore can you, because I heard you tell me that you love me. Isn't it time you just accepted it?"

I lifted my face to his, and we were seconds away from our first kiss, or at least the first one I remembered, when the Priscillas came flying down the hall. True to form they didn't stop but landed on both our heads. Pris pulled my hair, and Cil pulled Zeid's.

"Not now, people," Pris said. "Stuff to do. Move it."

Zeid and I gave each other one last look and then let ourselves be pulled away into the direction of our rooms. But this time I took with me the certain knowledge that Zeid and I were meant to be together and there was no more room for wondering about it.

Because Pris was right, we had too much to do to spend time mooning around at each other. There would be plenty of time for that later after we completed our mission.

Pris continued to push me down the hall towards my room. I wasn't surprised when she came into my room with me, too. I knew Pris planned to keep my mind off the fact that Beru wasn't there with me.

Pris didn't look, or even often act, as if she cared about anyone's feelings. But like Ruta, Pris was intensely aware of everything that was going on, including all our emotions. To do that, I knew that she had a deep well of love and compassion inside of her. She just showed it differently.

Less than an hour later we were all in the planning room, the three of us smelling much better. Leif was at the head of the table, with his staff resting once more in the corner of the room. I knew that he could summon it by thinking about it, that he had powers most of us didn't know about, but sitting there he gave none of that away.

It was Professor Link who asked the first question. It was to me. I was expecting it. He held up the button that I had pressed on to Zeid and said, "I gave this to you to use, not to stick on someone else."

I started to respond, but he held up his hand, "However, in this case, this was probably the wisest choice. You knew that Zeid could tell us what was going on and if necessary transport back there to help. So it was a wise tactical choice. But next time, you push it to get yourself home. Am I clear about that?"

I nodded and took the button and returned it to the spot where I had ripped it off. I hoped never to use it again. And even though I agreed, I wasn't so sure I wouldn't do the same thing again.

When I saw Link's eyes darken and squint at me, I knew he knew what I was thinking. But he moved on. As Pris said, we had quite a few things to address and fighting with me about what I would do was wasting time. Besides, I had questions.

"How did Abbadon stop us from using our magical powers? He must have done the same thing to the others before he trapped them."

I didn't want to mention that I was worried that he had used the thought-worms on them first. On the other hand, now that they knew how to get the worms out of people's heads, perhaps it wouldn't be fatal for them.

"Well, first he stopped us being able to communicate, so perhaps we should start there. How did he do it?" Link asked.

Pita looked at Teddy who waved his hand at him to continue. "It's probably the same thing. It's actually what we were going to use to jam the signals of the thought-worms."

"A disrupter like the ones you made for us?" I asked, probably a little too loudly. Okay, it was loud. I yelled it, and I kept on yelling. "How did that happen? Is there a spy like you thought before? How could he possibly be making the same thing? And then, zut it, he used it first!"

I stamped my foot, under the table. I didn't know what else to do with the anger that surged inside of me.

Everyone waited for me to calm down, then Pita added, "It won't happen again. We've developed a system that can't be hacked or disabled."

"How do you know it hasn't been stolen again? Have you caught the traitor?"

Leif stepped in, "Could we answer those questions for you later, Kara? Right now we need to rescue our people. All I can promise you is that all of you will have your powers and Link will be able to communicate with all of you without any disruption."

The fact that I didn't know how that was going to work bothered me, but I knew it was my need to control everything that made me upset. It was stupid. The people around the table were far more skilled than me. I needed to learn how to be quiet and do what I was told.

When I heard Zeid laughing beside me, I wanted to pinch his leg the way Beru pinched mine, but he was too quick for me. He grabbed my hand and held it while we listened to the rest of how we were going to rescue the villagers and our people.

Didn't sound too hard. Kidding. It scared the pants off of me.

FIFTY FOUR

Before the meeting broke up, we all thanked Earl and Ariel for the wall of water they had dumped on us. Earl explained that as soon as Zeid returned and they learned what was happening, they didn't waste any time. They knew that water was a disruption that Abbadon couldn't counter. Abbadon doesn't have nature on his side.

The rain stopped the worm's sensors from finding us. As we had seen when the dragons pulled us away, the thought-worms became disoriented, and the worm trees toppled over.

"What happened after that? What happened to the worms?"

"The Priscillas' friends happened to the worms," Earl responded, laughing his big booming laugh.

"What friends? What did they do to the worms?"

"They ate them," La said, almost tripping over her feet as she spun around in delight.

"What could possibly eat them?" I asked, thinking of the rubbery surface and the computer parts inside.

"Goats!" La yelled. "Goats! They said they could and they would. And they did. It was awesome."

"Yup!" Cil added. "We have goat teams all over Zerenity looking for those ugly buggers. By the time they're done, there won't be any thought-worms left anywhere. Of course, we can't leave them unsupervised, otherwise they would eat other stuff that perhaps the villagers would prefer them not to eat, like gardens."

"And furniture and clothes," La added, still laughing.

I stared at the three of them, and couldn't believe they had come up with such a simple solution. "But are you going to tell me that you move the goats to different places using Sound Bubbles?"

"Oh, that would be silly, wouldn't it?" La said. "All those little goat feet flying over Zerenity."

"Well then, how are you getting them there?" I asked, almost pouting because I thought they were teasing me and this was no time to be teasing.

Teddy held up his hand. I stared at him like he was crazy. "What are you holding your hand up for, Teddy?"

"I have the answer!"

"Zounds, is everyone wacko today? How? Just tell me!"

"Goat tunnels. Well, not tunnels so much as something that moves a subway in the Earth Realm."

"You are moving goats through subways underground? Goat trains?"

"Oh, that's a good one. Yes. Goat trains. Moves them fast, keeps them contained."

I put my forehead down on the table. This was too much. Goat trains. But then I started thinking about what that would look like—goats popping up and down in the countryside like whack-a-moles—and I started laughing too. Soon we were all laughing so hard the cups of water and coffee on the table almost fell off from the vibrations.

A few minutes later, after wiping the tears off my face, I said, "Oh, I needed that!"

Leif nodded. "We all needed that. Laughter and joy are another weapon we have that Abbadon does not."

We were still smiling as we left the planning room heading to where we needed to go. We were mentally adjusting to our next mission. We all had a different one, but each task would be working in harmony with the whole.

Niko, Zeid, and I were to free the villagers frozen in time and space.

Others were handling the mental virus called Deadsweep. There was a whole kingdom to clean, but we knew how to do it now.

Reports of violence taking place in villages all over Zerenity had come in, but teams of Whistle Pigs, Ginete, and the goats were going to every one of them.

The Ginete and Whistle Pigs were using the same techniques that we had used at the schoolhouse. They brought with them the drones to test people, and technology that would disrupt the signals from Abbadon to the thought-worms and the sensors within them. The hardest part was stunning the infected without hurting them.

Since I couldn't go with them, Pita was using a version of the sound signals that the Shrieks had used against us. Abbadon had provided us with that idea, and we were using it. It was a terrible weapon, but we weren't using it that way. It was safer than gas and, using the correct decimals no one would suffer any damaging effects from it.

Once the team contained each village, Leif and Sarah would transport there and reverse any mental damage that the worms may have caused to the people. They were using the same idea on them that we were going to use to rescue the frozen villages.

On the individuals, there was always the chance that what they were doing would send them into insanity. Lock them into a place from which we could never rescue them. That's why Leif and Sarah were doing it. They wanted to take full responsibility. In case something went wrong, it would be only their fault.

But Kinver was ours to rescue. However, before we did, we had to find the one person who could help us. The person who understood portals better than anyone else. Who had traveled back and forth between the Earth and Erda dimensions for years. Who had lived in both places without disrupting the time continuum in either one. We had to find Suzanne. That was the first step. We were going to Eiddwen.

As we headed to where the Sound Bubble was waiting for us, I asked the question everyone was thinking, "What if that village is frozen too?"

"It could be worse," Niko said. "They could all be dead."

No one said anything. Niko was right. They could be. I thought I had prepared for anything: tree worms, destroyed villages, or frozen villagers. But the one thing I hadn't thought of was what we found.

It was worse than I could have imagined.

FIFTY FIVE

We smelled it before we saw it. Not the smell of worms. That would have been much better. The air was rancid, dense, and filled with ash and the smell of fire.

Afraid that it would alert the wrong people to our arrival, we had decided not to take the Sound Bubble. Instead, Zeid transported us back to the forest outside of Eiddwen. I couldn't believe that only a week had passed since the day I decided to leave Eiddwen and walk back to the Castle.

It had only been a week since I had seen the silver trail and followed it out of the village where I found Cahir waiting at the edge of the forest.

He was waiting for us now. Even if I hadn't smelled the smoke, I would have known something was terribly wrong. As calm as Cahir usually was, this time, he wasn't. He was pacing back and forth and growled when he saw us arrive out of nowhere.

Did he think that what happened was our fault? Because of how many days it had taken for us to get here?

"Stay here," Niko said to all of us.

No one obeyed. Ruta, Zeid, Cahir, and I walked behind Niko until we stopped on the hill that looked down onto the village below. The last time we had looked at this view together, Aki and Beru were with us. We had marveled at the crystal blue sky and thought how lucky we were to be together on such a beautiful day.

Now we had no idea what had happened to Aki, or if we could save Beru. And instead of a beautiful village, there was nothing. Just a black, burned out wasteland.

I fell to my knees and screamed. I screamed so loud I was sure the hawks circling in the sky overhead heard me. I screamed as I started running, calling out for my father, Berta, Suzanne, and Aki.

Niko and Zeid tried to grab me and stop me, but I ran the way that Beru had taught me. I breathed in the power of the earth; I reached out to the trees and let their energy flow to me. I ran faster than the wind. Even Cahir couldn't stop me.

I ran until I reached the village and then the reality of what had happened stopped me. There was nothing left. Blackened beams jutted up into the sky. Large pieces of burnt wood littered the street. There was nothing. All the people I had met who had been so kind to me, were gone.

Was I responsible for this? Was it because this was our hometown? Did Abbadon hate us that much? I knew who had burned the village. I didn't know how, but I knew that Abbadon was responsible. He was responsible for taking away my family's home town, for the homes and lives of all the people who lived here.

I screamed and screamed until there was nothing left inside of me. Niko, Zeid, Ruta, and Cahir stood beside me, tears running down their faces. It was okay. I had screamed for them, too.

When there was nothing left, I turned away, ready to leave, when Niko grabbed my arm.

"Do you give up this easily? Are you still just that little girl who returned from Earth? Have you not learned anything at all?"

I pulled my arm away and yelled, "How dare you! They are all gone. My father is dead. Abbadon won here. Don't you get it? We lost. And now, without Suzanne, we have lost Kinver too. What good did your training do here? None!"

Niko slapped me.

I started to slap him back, but Zeid caught my arm. I was so furious by then I was ready to hit Zeid and maybe kick Ruta, but I caught a glimpse of Cahir looking at me, and I realized what I was doing.

"Zut! Am I infected? Oh, my gods. I need to go back to the Castle and have Leif take this out of me."

"Stop it, Kara Beth," Zeid hissed. "You are not infected with anything except your own self-importance. Do you think all of us don't feel what you are feeling? Grow up. Niko is right. Haven't you learned anything?"

Seeing Zeid mad at me did something. I sat down on the road and put my head between my knees and cried.

I didn't deserve it, but they waited for me, and when I was done crying I stood up and forced out the words, "So, you aren't as upset as me. What am I missing?"

"We are upset, Kara, but you are right, not in the same way. Yes, the village is gone. But what is wrong with this picture? What do you see besides burned buildings?"

"Nothing," I whined.

No one said anything. Then it dawned on me. "Wait, I don't see any bodies. Wouldn't there be bodies somewhere?"

Suddenly, a whiff of hope flew through me. "If there are no bodies, where are the people?"

At that point, having them frozen like the people in Kinver sounded pretty good compared to everyone dying in the fire.

Zeid nodded at the star I wore around my neck. I understood. I needed to see what was invisible to our regular sight.

Before I pressed it though, I had a horrifying thought. I remembered using the star before and seeing hundreds of Shrieks surrounding us. What if I touched it now and saw millions of worms? Which was worse, seeing them or not seeing, or imagining them? It had to be imagining. I could almost feel them crawling on me as I thought about it.

At least I would be able to stop them if I knew they were there. Trembling, I lifted my hand to the star and pressed it. The world adjusted itself, and the picture I couldn't see before appeared in front of me. No, the villagers weren't frozen. They weren't there at all.

While the vision lasted, I walked through the village, the black ashes coating my feet and legs. No walls were left standing, and seeing that blackness in 4D made the destruction a thousand times worse. But still, there was no sign of life.

With only a few minutes left before my sight changed back to 3D, I made it to where I thought my father's house had been. I thought of Berta and how organized she was. Everything in place. She knew what was happening at all times. Did she know that the fire was coming and that Abbadon would target this village differently?

If she did, I asked myself, what would she have done? Standing in the hallway where I had hugged Berta goodbye, I looked down at the blackened floor and saw what Berta had done. And that's when I knew where Aki, Suzanne, and Berta had taken the village.

FIFTY SIX

"The trouble is, I don't know how to get them back, or tell them to come home," I said to Niko, Zeid, and Ruta. They had seen me whoop in excitement, so they knew I had seen something, but they were still trying to follow what I was telling them.

"Back up, Kara," Niko said. "Because you saw something that you believe Berta left for you, you think that the village is still here? Where?"

Niko spread his arms out, taking in the blackened, ash-filled village. "Where would they be if they were here?"

"Well, they are not actually here. They are here and there. And I think I am going to need help to contact them."

Of course, Professor Link had been listening into the conversation, so he asked, "What kind of help do you need?"

"Suzanne had once told me there are people in Erda who have traveled to more dimensions than just Earth and Erda. Dimension travelers. I need one or two of them, please. And I need them yesterday, if you know what I mean."

"Hum, okay, give me a minute and let me see if I can find you one," Link said.

I turned to the three of them, looking at me as if I had lost my mind, and said, "You know what I wish?"

"Besides, a dead Abbadon, Deadsweep eliminated from the face of the planet, everyone returned unharmed, and oh, maybe a shower?" Zeid said, pointing at my blackened state.

"Yes, besides that. I wish I had a clean place to sit. Like a rock." Before I finished speaking, I sat down—on a rock that hadn't been there the moment before.

"Wow," Zeid said. "When did you figure out how to do that?"

"Not that long ago. I didn't do anything. The rock was already here before I asked for it. But because I saw it during the 4D time, I could aim myself right above it and sit on it. I'm trying to make a point here. I think that is what is going on with the village. They are all still here. But not.

"I think that somehow one of them, or maybe all three, opened a giant portal and shoved everyone in there before the fire swept through the town. But I don't think Suzanne opened the other end of the portal because she wants them all to stay in the Erda dimension. They are inside something that is an in-between place. Like a waiting room."

"But how do you know this? Did you see them?" Zeid asked.

"No. That's the thing. I don't know how to move between dimensions. Suzanne pushed me through the portal to get to Erda. So I couldn't see the people, but I did see something that made me think that what I am saying is true."

"What?" Niko asked.

I pointed down to what used to be the floor of my father's house. "Look closely. What do you see?"

I waited patiently while the three of them looked and looked. "Okay, cross your eyes or something. Expect to see it."

"Zounds," Niko said. "A silver thread... going up into the air and then it disappears."

"Exactly," I said. "Where do you think the other end of that silver thread goes?"

Link broke in just about the time everyone said, "Oh!"

"Found someone. Actually, I found two of them. Well, I didn't find them, Pita did. He said they were old friends of his. Well, not friends so much as someone he drinks with, and that's how he knew they were dimension travelers. All the stories they tell. Sorry, rambling. Not like me. Anyway, they are on their way to you now."

I didn't even have time to ask how they were arriving when Leif popped into view holding the hands of two ordinary looking people. I don't know what I expected. Ghosts? These two looked so much like each other, I thought they might be siblings.

"Thought I would bring them to you," Leif said. "I have had some experience traveling through the Earth to Erda portal, but these two youngsters seem to have been moving around for hundreds of years to many dimensions. Of course, since Abbadon had been active, all the portals are closed, so they claim to be a little rusty, but they know more than the rest of us."

The two "young people" laughed. The young woman spoke up, "We're not young, we just stopped our aging at twenty-five. We are both hundreds of Earth years old. I'm Anne and this is my twin brother, Garth. How can we help?"

I explained the situation to them. We thought the town was in the waiting room of a portal to somewhere. When I showed Anne and Garth the silver thread, they nodded at each other.

"Well, this should be easy. Since we have your permission, we can open the door to where the villagers are and let them all out. But do you want them to come out here in this?" Anne said waving her arm at the filth we were standing in.

"You can open the door anywhere?" When they nodded yes, I suggested the meadow.

The two of them held hands and vanished. A few minutes later we saw the strangest thing. Out in the middle of the meadow, people were stepping out of a hole in the air and onto the ground.

We started running, and we got there just in time to see Aki and Suzanne step out into the meadow. Right behind them was Berta.

And with her was a man who looked like my father, except he was walking.

"You're well," I squealed and ran into his arms.

"About time, don't you think?" he said.

I wanted to stay and find out everything, but we still had to free Kinver. We quickly caught Suzanne and Aki up with what we needed to do.

They both looked exhausted, especially Suzanne. For days, they had to keep both doors of the portal closed while trying to keep the people from the village from freaking out. Everyone was tired and hungry. Although before stepping into the portal, Suzanne had them all bring food, water, and clothes, the food had run out, and they were low on water.

Now, seeing their village burned to the ground, most of the villagers started to cry. It had been a beautiful village, and it was gone. Abbadon had burned it for no reason at all other than for spite.

However, there was some good news. Aki said that there had been no worms when they arrived. Perhaps Abbadon didn't want to bother with slow death for the village his brother called home. He wanted immediate and painful deaths for everyone.

What Abbadon hadn't counted on was Suzanne being there. He would be disappointed to discover the townspeople had survived and would rebuild.

"I'm going to stay here," Aki said. "We need to get food and water and shelter for the villagers. Berta, your father, and I can handle this, Kara. The rest of you go take care of Kinver."

"May we help?" Anne and Garth asked. Suzanne nodded. "I'm going to need help. From what you have told me, Kara Beth, Abbadon didn't just put them into a portal. He has frozen them in time and space. If we make a mistake, it could instantly kill them all."

FIFTY SEVEN

Leif took us to Kinver. He waved his staff over our little group and the next thing we knew we were standing back on the road we had been on the day before.

"That's a wizard for you," Zeid whispered to me. "I was exhausted after moving only four of us, and he just moved all of us with a flick of his wrist."

It was true. Leif looked as if nothing had happened, except maybe a brief stroll to the other side of a room.

"That's a pretty good description of it," Leif said. "It is like a stroll to the other side of a room."

"Do you need to wave the staff to make it happen?" I asked. "Or is that just theater?"

Leif laughed. "You decide. I need to get back to helping restore the infected. We can talk about that later."

I thought the question was kind of like asking me if I believed there was a Santa Claus. No. And then yes. Depended on how one saw the idea of it.

As soon as we arrived, the twins went into a huddle with Suzanne.

That left Zeid, Niko, and I waiting for instructions. Waiting was hard. I wanted to be doing something, anything. But locked portals and villages that were frozen in time and space was not something my magic could fix, at least not without help.

Usually, I would hug Cahir to calm myself down, but Cahir wasn't with us. He refused to be transported around by anyone, even a wizard. So I had sent him off to check on his family since there wasn't anything he could do at Kinver

"Go now," I had whispered to him, "But don't stay long. We have to go get Abbadon."

He hadn't wasted a moment. He gave me a chance to give him a brief hug and then he ran off towards his home. I knew he would meet me back at the Castle once he had checked on his family.

Family. These people were my family. Kinver was a home for me. It was where I could be Hannah. Not Princess Kara Beth. Just a beloved daughter. I needed them back.

Suzanne and the twins called us over. "We think we know what to do. Could you describe it one more time for us, or even better, could you show us?"

"Show you? How could I do that?" I asked. I turned to Ruta. "You knew that they were here. Can't you see them?"

"No. I just felt them with the help of the trees."

"Honestly, I don't know how to show you," I said. "I used this star to refocus the way I see the world. And in the 4D viewpoint, I could see the town. Everyone was frozen. Dark threads were running through the air all around them. Since they were frozen, I don't know if they could see me, except for Liza. She's the girl who gave me this star because she can see 4D without it. Liza projected the word 'portal' into the air for me to see."

Garth spoke up, "That's perfect. The word portal is all we needed to know. We thought that was what has happened. They are in a portal the way the people in Eiddwen were, but Abbadon opened this one and stuck them there.

"But we think that we can get them out. As you know, portals between dimensions manipulate time and space. Neither of which are linear, even though it appears that way to us.

"That's why we can travel to many dimensions which are operating in what you might call different time zones and return to this dimension, and it will be just as we left it."

Suzanne spoke up, "That's how I could travel between Earth and Erda which operate on a very different sense of time. The danger lies in the transporting. If something goes wrong, the person could be trapped somewhere in time, or pieces of themselves would disperse into many time zones.

"We are lucky in that Abbadon appears to have frozen the people of Kinver in time and space instead of dispersing them throughout the universes. They are in a place similar to the waiting room in the portal where we kept the village of Eiddwen.

"The difference is that he froze them there. That way he could keep them there forever, trapped between life and death. Perhaps he didn't know you would be able to see them. Or maybe he knew you would find them, but didn't think you would be able to unfreeze them without killing them in the process. That is the more likely scenario. He expected you to find them, try to unfreeze them, and then fail. That way you could feel guilty forever."

"But we won't fail. We do need you to take us there though," Suzanne said. "We need to use you as a marker. You are here, but you can see inside the portal. If you can hold the vision for long enough, we can find the opening to the portal, step inside, and let the villagers out."

"And if I can't? What will happen to you?"

"The same thing that will happen to the rest of the village. Either we will all be frozen forever, or dispersed in time and space."

"So if I fail, you die?" I whispered, fear creeping through every pore in my body.

"You won't fail," Suzanne said. I knew enough not to say anything. I needed all the encouragement I could get, and she was speaking it for herself as much as for me.

"One last thing. You said dark threads. Could those threads be worms strung together?"

The horror of what Suzanne said hit me like a sledgehammer. They could be worms. If we unfreeze the people, the thought-worms will be loose.

"We can handle that part, Kara Beth," Niko said. "We have the disrupters. Coro and Ariel can be called in. The villagers will be a little wet, but I don't think they'll mind. We have a drone to check if someone is already infected. And of course, the Priscillas will have the goats here.

"All you have to do is hold the vision so that Garth, Anne, and Suzanne can find the portal."

I looked around at everyone waiting expectantly. People who believed in me. I thought of the people waiting for us to free them, and said, "Okay, let's do it."

Suzanne, Anne, and Garth gathered around me. The twins held my hand, and Suzanne put her hands on my shoulder and said the same words she said to me the first time we went through a portal together. "Go, go, go."

I touched the star and showed them the village. All I had to do was hold that vision. I focused on Liza, knowing that if anyone could help me, she could.

I heard Anne whisper, "Wow," and then the world started to shatter.

FIFTY EIGHT

I groaned and tried to sit up. "What happened?" I asked, still struggling to open my eyes. Someone was helping me, but my eyes wouldn't open enough to see who it was. All my body wanted to do was lie back down and go to sleep.

The sweetest voice I had ever heard said, "You fainted."

My eyes flew open, and all sense of tiredness vanished. "Beru!" I yelled.

I didn't care if she didn't want me to hug her; I did it anyway. She was thinner and tired, but as beautiful as ever. Still holding on to her, I almost fell over my feet to get to James and Liza.

Tears streamed down my face as I saw that the entire village had returned. People were already in their homes, opening doors and windows. Children were laughing in the streets.

"The worms?"

"No worms," Suzanne said. "What looked like dark threads were cracks, like cracks in ice. Abbadon probably had to do the freezing quickly, which made it easier to release everyone because of the imperfections."

"Or else he did it on purpose," I mumbled under my breath. In my head, Link answered me, "You may be onto something, Kara Beth."

I should have been elated. But once the excitement of seeing Beru and the people of Kinver had faded, I found that what I felt was depressed. I think I hid it well, though.

Despite feeling depressed, or maybe because I was, I wouldn't let Beru out of my sight as we all circled through the village, making sure that everything was okay.

We spent a few minutes in James' home. His wife was busy making food and wanted us to stay, but we knew we couldn't. Something was still bothering me. Even though Deadsweep had been terrifying, and finding a burned village and a frozen village was horrible, it seemed as if we were missing something.

It had been hard, but easy at the same time. Almost like we were being played. Well, not almost. We were being played. We were responding time and time again to the manipulations of Abbadon. First his Shrieks and Shatterskin, then the Deadsweep infection of thought-worms, and finally the burning and freezing of whole towns.

We were always running after a problem to solve it when Abbadon was the real problem. We were going to have to change our tactics and go after him.

Even the idea of riding in the Sound Bubble didn't cheer me up. Preparing to say goodbye, I hugged everyone I could in the village one last time, with longer hugs for James and Liza. Liza had given us the answer, and I told her that she was the hero of the moment. She didn't say anything, just held my hands and told me she loved me and that all was well.

Liza was a wise girl, soon to be a wise woman. I had a feeling she would be playing a more significant part in finding Abbadon. When she winked at me, I realized she already knew that. I stayed longer in James' hug, being Hannah for a few minutes. That helped too.

The Sound Bubble arrived, and it helped a little bit. The harmony reached deep into my bones and vibrated through my blood, raising my spirits. Whoever had "invented" the Sound Bubble had done a wonderful thing.

Anne and Garth had their own bubble. They were returning home. We had all asked them to come to the Castle with us so that we could thank them officially for their help, but they refused, saying they needed to check on their village. Garth added that now that we knew where to find them, they did hope we would ask them to help again.

A second Sound Bubble descended over everyone except Suzanne and me. I thought it was a mistake and turned to ask Suzanne how we were getting back to the Castle. Instead of answering, Suzanne morphed into a dragon right before my eyes. No one in the village seemed surprised, but I still couldn't believe that kind of thing happened as an everyday occurrence. A dragon. I stood and looked at her, not sure what was happening.

Dolt that I am, it took a push from Liza to realize that I was going to ride back to the Castle on the dragon, on Lady. A bolt of happiness shot through me. It was just what I needed. A dragon ride. A dragon ride with no danger. Just the joy of flying. James had run back into the house and got a harness for me, but I shook my head. I was going to hold on. I could do it. I was Princess Kara Beth, dragon rider.

Lady bent down, and I hopped on, tucking my legs in the crease of her wings and holding onto the red comb of feathers on her head. They were soft, so I could lie in them and hold onto her head that way if I needed to. But I had a feeling that Lady was going to take me on a leisurely trip and I wanted to see everything.

Lady slowly flapped her wings, everyone stepping back to give her space, and lifted into the air with the same grace I had seen my pileated woodpeckers in the Earth dimension have. To my delight, as we rose, I saw that other dragons were waiting for us. We were going to fly together.

Nothing could have prepared me for the glory of that ride. Lady took her time. We flew over villages and mountains. At times I was cold, but the joy I felt overrode any discomfort. I was part of something so much bigger than myself. I was a dot of a person flying on a dragon within the midst of a mighty crown of other dragons.

The sky was vast, the sun played hide and seek in the clouds, and the land below us was fertile and green. Coro arranged a little storm for us off in the distance so that I could see its full majesty. Ariel gave us a tiny push of wind once in a while and played with the tree leaves as we passed over the old growth forests of Erda.

The whole experience was like a dream. A beautiful dream. I knew that was Lady and her dragon friends' intention. They wanted to give me back my hope and joy. It worked. When the roof of the atrium opened, and Lady and I dropped down onto the practice field, I felt like a new person.

We had prevailed. Beauty and goodness were the King and Queen of the Kingdom of Zerenity, and I had the privilege of keeping it that way. Nothing else had changed, but I had a new viewpoint, and that made all the difference.

FIFTY NINE

The Castle was in full celebration mode. Suzanne and I could hear the laughter before we even touched down. By the time we made it to the atrium, we felt re-energized just from all the happiness weaving its way through the Castle.

Beru was waiting for us. We slid our hands and wiggled our fingers in our familiar salute to each other and walked hand in hand to the table where everyone was already seated having dinner together. It had been a long day.

I patted George, the metal toadstool, on the head, and he skipped a step almost knocking the drinks that he was carrying off his tray.

Once I found my seat beside Zeid, I asked, "Where is Aki?"

"She and Berta, along with your father, are supervising the rebuilding of Eiddwen. We've already sent a group of workmen to help, but it will take a while. Of course, a little magic here and there will make it go faster," Professor Link answered.

"Are you planning to visit?" I asked, knowing full well that Professor Link didn't like traveling. He knew I was asking if he was going to miss Aki personally. When he answered, "I will," we both knew what he meant.

After lunch, and a brief visit to our bedrooms to get cleaned up, we all met back in the planning room. We knew that there was one more mystery to solve. It would have been so easy not to do anything and wait until the next crisis, pretending that the bigger problem was over, but all of us knew what was at stake.

Once we were all settled, with the Priscillas sitting on the edge of the table in front of me, Niko stated the problem.

"This is what we needed to know. Who delivered the walking sticks? Who was the spy in our midst, and are they still here?"

"Since you used the past tense—needed to know—does this mean you have the answer?" Zeid asked.

"Yes, I do. And the answer is disturbing, to say the least," Niko answered.

"Oh, let me guess," I said trying not to be sarcastic and failing miserably. "It was Abbadon."

A chorus of astonishment and disbelief went around the room.

"No, it couldn't have been," Zeid said. "We would have known. Besides he lives thousands of miles away in some castle, locked away all by himself."

"That's what he has wanted us to believe, and we all fell for it," Niko replied. "Instead, he was here, working in the Castle."

An appalled silence fell over the room. The idea that the man who had been causing all the death and destruction had been with us the whole time was too hard, and too awful, to contemplate. After what seemed like an eternity, and when no one asked the next question, I did. I had something to tell them, but first I wanted to hear what Niko had to say.

"How did you find out?"

Niko nodded at Link, and he took over.

"While you were all out taking care of the mess that Abbadon was making, I spent some time personally talking to every member of the staff. Eventually, I discovered that a person was working in the Castle that everyone saw once in a while, but had no idea what he did, or where he came from.

"The problem was, no one said anything. They let it go, thinking that it wasn't important. But once I started asking around, it became obvious it was someone who wasn't supposed to be here. When I started putting the timing together, I discovered that the unknown person had left about the same time the Deadsweep infection began."

"Walking down the road as a tradesman selling walking sticks," I said.

"Exactly," Niko answered.

"One problem. Well probably more than one problem, but there is something that doesn't make sense. How could Abbadon have made Deadsweep thought-worms while working in the Castle?" Ruta asked.

"Or if he was here all along, how did he make the Shrieks and Shatterskin?" Beru chimed in.

Niko shook his head. "That's something I don't have an answer for. Perhaps he made them all before he came to work here. Maybe he stored the walking sticks here until he was ready to release them. Or someone else brought them to him."

"Or that." Link responded.

Listening to everyone, I wasn't sure if I was getting depressed or angry. I decided it would be better if I got angry. That way I might be able to do something. I could feel the depression creeping in, making me feel like going to bed, curling up in a ball, and pulling the covers over my head.

In the end, what good would that do? Abbadon would still be out there. He would invent another thing that we would have to fight. The whole ziffering mess would start over again.

It was Zeid who asked the question I didn't feel like answering.

"How did you know that Abbadon was here, Kara Beth? You weren't surprised by what Niko said, so you must have known. Did you?"

Everyone turned to look at me as if I had an answer for them. As if I was magic or something, and could tell them the answer to all the questions, and then fix the mess too. I didn't have anything other than a piece of paper that I had kept clutched in my hand from the moment I had found it.

Instead of answering, I opened my hand and let the crumpled paper fall out onto the table. Zeid looked at me with both love and pain in his eyes and picked up the paper. Opening it, he read out loud, "See you soon, Princess Kara Beth. To our future together. Abbadon."

"Where did you get this?" Zeid whispered.

I dropped my head, afraid to look up, and whispered back, "It was on my bed when I went back to my bedroom."

The room erupted. Everyone was talking at once. Link left the room, and we waited for him to come back. Zeid had pulled me close, and I gave in and let my head rest on his shoulder. Really, at the moment I had no fight left in me.

When Link returned, we stopped talking and waited to hear what he had to tell us. We knew where he had gone.

"I checked with the staff. Every day someone went into your bedroom and cleaned it, waiting for your return, Kara Beth. So if you found the note today, it was placed there today, after you left."

"Which means," Zeid continued, "That either Abbadon came back, never left, or he has people working for him in the Castle."

SIXTY

We were back, standing on the bluff overlooking Eiddwen. The last time we had stood here we had found a burned-out village. Now, only a week later, everything that had been burned had been cleared away. Even from where we were standing, we could see the shells of homes going up all over the village.

Eiddwen was bustling with villagers helping each other rebuild homes and gardens. Their time trapped in the portal seemed to have renewed their spirits. We had heard reports of people going back to their gifts of magic and skills and practicing again.

Their joy and happiness were contagious. The closer we got to the village, the happier I felt, and I knew Zeid felt the same way. We were walking hand in hand as if we didn't have a care in the world, and that was the way I wanted to feel for as long as possible.

The ever-resourceful Ginete had supplied tents, and that's where everyone was living until they finished their homes. We were heading to the tent at the edge of town. The only way I knew it was my father's tent was the small flag flying from the point at the top of the tent. Otherwise, it looked the same as everyone else's. That too made me happy. We were part of a community. Perhaps responsible for its wellbeing, but not above it.

Zeid and I were there to say goodbye. Everyone else in the team, including Aki, had gone to say goodbye to their friends and family, too. We weren't waiting for the next disaster. We were being proactive and going after Abbadon before he unleashed another catastrophe on the kingdom. That's what we told people. But we weren't naïve. We were sure he knew we were coming, and had already planned on how to stop us.

My father was standing at the open flap of the tent waiting for us. I let go of Zeid's hand and flew into his arms. It had been so long since he had truly hugged me. It had been lifetimes for me in the Earth Realm, and now almost a year in Erda.

When I had returned to Erda, I didn't remember my Erda parents. What made it worse was my mom had died in a Shatterskin attack and my father fell into such a deep depression everyone thought he would die. There had been no happy reunion then. I was ready for it now.

Berta was standing behind my father, and I fell into her arms too while Zeid and Darius did the male patting each other on the back kind of hug.

The next few days were heaven. Berta pampered us all with delicious food. Zeid and I worked with the villagers to help rebuild their homes. I was thrilled to find that every friend that I had made while staying in Eiddwen had made it through Deadsweep unharmed.

At night, Zeid and I sat with Berta and Darius and listened to them tell tales about the Kingdom of Zerenity.

What I most wanted was to gather my father's knowledge of Abbadon. But he didn't know much more than I did. They had never been brothers that lived together. If Aki's story was true, both had been set in their separate Kingdoms by the bored brothers on the snake-space ship. I knew Aki had more stories to tell about those bored brothers from outer space. I wondered if they had ever come to visit again to see how their experiment had gone.

But since my father knew so little, I put those thoughts away. I could wait and talk to Aki. Instead, I listened and immersed myself in what Berta and Darius had to share about the villagers, the Kingdom, and my mother.

I let it fill me up so that it could carry me across the shattered lands and trees into Abbadon's desert kingdom. Link had winked at me before we left and whispered to me that we were going to travel in a different way this time. But he wouldn't tell me how. Link loved preparing surprises and took every chance he could to do so. I was happy to let him surprise me. I like surprises, as long as they are pleasant surprises.

The day Cahir came to the village walking down the street without a care in the world and everyone smiled and waved at him, was one of those surprises. I had no idea that everyone in Eiddwen knew Cahir.

Berta just laughed at me and said, "Of course, dear. He grew up here. Everyone knows and loves him."

Cahir's arrival meant one thing. It was time for us to go. Cahir showed me where his family was staying outside the village. I told Berta, and she promised to watch over them and make sure there was plenty for his family to eat.

After everyone said their goodbyes, and as the Sound Bubble came closer, Cahir took off at a loping pace. He would see us back at the Castle where our team would be ready to start our next adventure together.

I promised everyone that we would be back. It was a promise I intended to keep.

Author Note

When the idea of the *Return To Erda* series came to me, so did the titles of the three books in the series. They popped into my head and there was nothing I could do to dislodge them. So I went with the titles and then figured out what each book was about after that.

That meant that I knew that the title of this book was going to be Deadsweep. But I didn't know what the danger was going to be. What was Deadsweep?

While I pondered that question, there were more and more stories in the news about the terrible things people were doing to each other. Then I heard a Ted Talk given by the mother of one of the boys who was a shooter in the school killings in Columbine, Colorado, and it all came together for me.

She explained how she had recognized no clues, no warning signs, that her son was going to go to school, murder people, and then kill himself. The mental illness that caused it was invisible to her.

How does this heart-breaking thing happen? And her story is not unique. This disease is often not visible to most of us until it is too late to stop it.

I know there is not an easy human answer to this illness. In Deadsweep, I talk about healing the rifts that we find in ourselves and between ourselves. Perhaps healing divisions between people would help stop the mental illness that can produce such horrifying results. It can't hurt, and it might help.

The other thing on my mind while writing some of the chapters about the infection called Deadsweep was the idea of contagion. For a week I had a cold. I was miserable. I would write for thirty minutes and fall asleep for another fifteen. Ugh. Plus, I was irritable.

I asked myself, was I irritable before I felt sick? Which came first? What if I got sick because I allowed myself to be irritated? Or what if infections were manufactured? What then?

Between those two ideas, mental illness and infections, Deadsweep as thought-worms that infected people's behavior, was born.

In the end, this is a fantasy book. I get to make up worlds, and people, and even the evil things that threaten that world. And then I get to make sure that evil never wins.

My desire is to tell a good story, but if the story also shifts perception along the way, it's an added bonus for me. I hope it is for you too.

If you would like to read a short prequel to both these series, I'll send it to you for free.

It answers a few questions about the brothers who seeded Earth and Erda, and a bit about where Suzanne really came from.

I'll tell you a secret: Earl and Ariel are not Suzanne's blood parents. And she has a sister Meg. More mystery. And another series, The Chronicles of Thamon.

Get this free short story here: becalewis.com/fantasy.

Happy Reading! Beca

Instagram: http://instagram.com/becalewis

LinkedIn: https://linkedin.com/in/becalewis

Acknowlegments

I could never write a book without the help of my friends and my book community. Thank you Jet Tucker, Jamie Lewis, Diana Cormier, and Barbara Budan for taking the time to do the final reader proof. You can't imagine how much I appreciate it.

A huge thank you to Laura Moliter for her fantastic book editing.

Thank you to every other member of my street team who helps me make so many decisions that help the book be the best book possible.

Thank you to all the people who tell me they love to read these stories. Those random comments from friends and strangers are more valuable than gold.

And always, thank you to my beloved husband, Del, for being my daily sounding board, for putting up with all my questions, my constant need to want to make things better, and for being the love of my life, in more than just this one lifetime.

ALSO BY BECA

The Rivers of Time Series: Women's Lit, Friendship, Small Town, Mystery, Magical Realism, Small Town Fiction
The Returning, The Awakening, The Rising

***Follow Me Here:* Women's Lit, Friendship, Small Town, Mystery, Magical Realism, Small Town Fiction**

The Ruby Sisters Series: Women's Lit, Friendship, Mystery, Small Town Fiction
A Last Gift, After All This Time, And Then She Remembered, As If It Was Real, Almost Innocent

Stories From Doveland: Women's Lit, Friendship, Small Town, Mystery, Magical Realism, Small Town Fiction
Karass, Pragma, Jatismar, Exousia, Stemma, Paragnosis, In-Between, Missing, Out Of Nowhere

The Return To Erda Series: Fantasy
Shatterskin, Deadsweep, Abbadon, The Experiment

The Chronicles of Thamon: Fantasy
Banished, Betrayed, Discovered, Wren's Story

The Shift Series: Spiritual Self-Help
Living in Grace: The Shift to Spiritual Perception
The Daily Shift: Daily Lessons From Love To Money
The 4 Essential Questions: Choosing Spiritually Healthy Habits
The 28 Day Shift To Wealth: A Daily Prosperity Plan
The Intent Course: Say Yes To What Moves You
Imagination Mastery: A Workbook For Shifting Your Reality
Right Thinking: A Thoughtful System for Healing
Perception Mastery: Seven Steps To Lasting Change
Blooming Your Life: How To Experience Consistent Happiness

Perception Parables: Very short stories
Love's Silent Sweet Secret: A Fable About Love
Golden Chains And Silver Cords: A Fable About Letting Go

Advice / Journals
A Woman's ABC's of Life: Lessons in Love, Life, and Career from Those Who Learned The Hard Way
The Daily Nudge(s): So When Did You First Notice

About Beca

Beca writes books she hopes will change people's perceptions of themselves and the world, and open possibilities to things and ideas that are waiting to be seen and experienced.

At sixteen, Beca founded her own dance studio. Later, she received a Master's Degree in Dance in Choreography from UCLA and founded the Harbinger Dance Theatre, a multimedia dance company, while continuing to run her dance school.

After graduating—to better support her three children—Beca switched to the sales field, where she worked as an employee and independent contractor in many industries, excelling in each while perfecting and teaching her Shift System and writing books.

She joined the financial industry in 1983 and became an Associate Vice President of Investments at a major stock brokerage firm. She was a licensed Certified Financial Planner for over twenty years.

This diversity, along with a variety of life challenges, helped fuel the desire to share what she's learned by writing and speaking, hoping it will make a difference in other people's lives.

Beca grew up in State College, PA, with the dream of becoming a dancer and then a writer. She carried that dream forward as she fulfilled a childhood wish by moving to Southern California in 1968. Beca told her family she would never move back to the cold.

After living there for thirty-one years, she met her husband, Delbert Lee Piper, Sr., at a retreat in Virginia, and everything changed. They decided to find a place they could call their own, which sent them off traveling around the United States. They lived and worked in a few different places before returning to live in the cold once again near Del's family in a small town in Northeast Ohio, not too far from State College.

When not working and teaching together, they love to visit and play with their combined family of eight children and five grandchildren, walk, read, study, do yoga or taiji, feed birds, and work in their garden.